The Journey Begins

A Kaya Classic
Volume 1

by Janet Shaw

★ American Girl®

Published by American Girl Publishing
Copyright © 2002, 2014 American Girl

Questions or comments? Call 1-800-845-0005,
visit **americangirl.com**, or write to Customer Service,
American Girl, 8400 Fairway Place, Middleton, WI 53562.

Printed in China
14 15 16 17 18 19 20 LEO 10 9 8 7 6 5 4 3 2 1

Cover image by Michael Dwornik and Juliana Kolesova

Cataloging-in-Publication Data available from the Library of Congress

Beforever

Beforever is about making connections.
It's about exploring the past, finding your
place in the present, and thinking about the
possibilities your future can bring. And it's about
seeing the common thread that ties girls from
all times together. The inspiring characters you
will meet stand up for what they care about
most: Helping others. Protecting the earth.
Overcoming injustice. Through their courageous
stories, discover how staying true to your own
beliefs will help make your world better
today—and tomorrow.

*To the Nez Perce girls and boys,
mothers and fathers, grandmothers and grandfathers,
unto the seventh generation*

*For my daughter, Laura Beeler, for Don Read,
and for my granddaughter, Maya Rain Beeler Balassa,
with love*

*For my son, Mark, his wife, Sue,
and their boys, Sam and Max,
with love*

TABLE *of* CONTENTS

Kaya and her family are *Nimíipuu*, known today as Nez Perce Indians. They speak the Nez Perce language, so you'll see some Nez Perce words in this book. "Kaya" is short for the Nez Perce name *Kaya'aton'my'*, which means "she who arranges rocks." You'll find the meanings and pronunciations of these and other Nez Perce words in the glossary on page 172.

Let's Race!

hen Kaya and her family rode over the hill into *Wallowa*, The Valley of the Winding Waters, her horse pricked up her ears and whinnied. Answering whinnies came from the large herd grazing nearby. Kaya stroked the smooth shoulder of her horse.

"Go easy, Steps High," she said softly. "We'll be there soon." But Steps High whinnied again and began to prance, stepping high just like her name. Speaking Rain's old pony whinnied, too. A sickness in Speaking Rain's eyes had caused her to lose her sight, so Kaya held the lead rope of her pony.

"I hear so many horses!" Speaking Rain said. "What do you see, Kaya? Tell me." Because Speaking Rain's parents had died, she'd lived with Kaya's family and was a sister to her.

Kaya studied the white-peaked mountains, the broad valley, and the shining lake so she could share the beauty of this beloved place with her blind sister.

"The snow's still deep on the mountains," Kaya said. "The lake reflects the green hills and the blue sky. The river's full of red salmon and running higher than I've ever seen it. The tepees are set far back from the bank."

"Where is everyone?" Speaking Rain asked. She held her buckskin doll against her chest.

"Some men are spearfishing in the river," Kaya said. "Some little boys are tossing up a hoop and trying to shoot arrows through it. Little girls are playing near the tepees, and all along the shore women are cleaning and drying salmon."

"I've smelled the salmon for a long time," Speaking Rain said. "It's a powerful scent! The men must have a big catch this year."

It was midsummer, the season when the salmon swam upstream to the lake to lay their eggs. Many bands of *Nimíipuu* gathered here each year to catch and dry the salmon. Kaya and her family were traveling with several other families from Salmon

River Country to join the fishing. Her family was also
visiting her father's parents. Kaya loved these reunions
with her grandparents and her many other relatives,
old and young—all the children were just like brothers
and sisters to each other.

Kaya's mother and her older sister, Brown Deer,
rode just ahead. Her mother glanced back over her
shoulder, then reined in her horse and motioned for
Brown Deer and Kaya to do the same.

"What is it, *Eetsa*?" Kaya asked her mother.

"The bundles on my pack horse have slipped a
little. They'll rub a sore spot if I don't balance them
again," Eetsa said. "I need to retie them."

Eetsa and Brown Deer quickly slipped off their
horses and began untying some woven bags from
a pack horse. Wing Feather, one of Kaya's twin
brothers, had been riding behind Eetsa's saddle.
The other twin, Sparrow, rode behind Brown Deer's.
It had been a long journey, and the little boys were
restless. Kaya helped the twins down so they could
stretch their legs. The boys giggled as they scampered
to hide behind a travois and peeked over, their dark
eyes gleaming.

"Look after your brothers well," Eetsa told Kaya, as she always did. Eetsa and Brown Deer hung several woven bags of dried roots and dried buffalo meat on their saddle horns.

As they worked, they glanced eagerly at the tepees along the river. Kaya smiled to herself. She was thinking that Nimíipuu loved to travel, but they loved the excitement of arrival even more. Already her grandfather and two of her uncles were riding out to greet them.

"I'm so glad we're here!" Brown Deer said. She smoothed her buckskin dress and touched the abalone shells she wore in her ears. "Remember what fun we had the last time we visited?"

Kaya nodded. *"Aa-heh!* I remember what fun you had dancing every night! I wonder which boys will serenade you this time," she teased. After the hard work came hours of trading and games. There would be feasting, singing, and always dancing, with the beat of the drums echoing down the valley.

Kaya turned and saw her father gazing at the herd of sleek horses, some of them spotted, in the wide meadow. Perhaps *Toe-ta* was thinking of trading for some of the horses, or of the races they'd have. He was an expert horseman. Often he won races on his fleet-footed stallion.

Kaya was certainly thinking about horse races. For a long time she'd imagined being in one on her adored Steps High. She knew Steps High was fast, but also young and untested. Toe-ta had told her that Steps High wasn't ready to race yet.

When Eetsa was satisfied that everything was in order, she and Brown Deer mounted their horses. Kaya helped the little boys climb back onto the patient animals and take their places again.

When Kaya turned to Steps High, the horse tossed her head and pawed the ground. Kaya rubbed her cheek against Steps High's soft muzzle. "If only we could race I know we'd win!" she whispered as she climbed into the saddle.

"Did you say something to me?" Speaking Rain asked, as Kaya took her pony's lead rope again.

"I was talking to Steps High," Kaya said. "I told her that when we race we'll beat all the others!"

Eetsa turned to look Kaya in the eye. "I've told you before not to boast," she said firmly. "Our actions speak for us. Our deeds show our worth. Let that be your lesson, Kaya."

Kaya pressed her lips together—she knew Eetsa was right.

"Come, let's meet the others," Toe-ta said, and led the way on his stallion.

When Kaya and her family rode up, her grand-mother, *Aalah*, and one of her aunts were waiting at the doorway of their tepee. Aalah stepped forward. Her face was creased with age, and little pockmarks, like fingerprints, covered her cheeks.

"*Tawts may-we!*" she said. "Welcome, my son! Welcome, all of you!" Smiling, she hugged Kaya and Speaking Rain as soon as they climbed off their horses. Then she took the twins into her arms. She kissed their chubby cheeks and tugged their braids.

"Tawts may-we!" Eetsa said. As Toe-ta and the others dismounted and shared greetings, she took the woven bags from her saddle horn. "We brought these for you," she said, offering their gifts with pleasure—it was an honor to give them.

Aalah received the gifts with thanks. Then Auntie put one hand on Kaya's shoulder and her other hand on Speaking Rain's. "You've grown! Are you hard workers like your sister, Brown Deer?"

"Aa-heh! We are!" Kaya and Speaking Rain said at the same time, and giggled.

"*Tawts!*" Auntie nodded. "You girls help Brown Deer unpack the horses and bring your things inside."

Kaya and Brown Deer carried their bundles into the tepee and placed them across from where their grandparents slept. Speaking Rain stacked the bundles neatly along the wall of the tepee. It was always packed full when they gathered here. But Kaya liked it crowded and cozy, and the tule mats that covered the tepee let in cool breezes and light.

After the women and girls had put everything in order around the tepee, Eetsa allowed Kaya to take Speaking Rain and the little boys to play. "Remember, it's your job to look after your brothers carefully," she reminded Kaya.

Kaya knew there were dangerous animals about. She also knew about the Stick People—small, mischievous people who might lure a child to wander

too far away into the woods. "Aa-heh," Kaya said.
"I will."

She led Speaking Rain and the twins to a group of
boys and girls gathered in the shade beside the river.
Raven, a boy a little older than Kaya, was playing a
game with a length of hemp cord.

"Here's what happened when Coyote went to put
up his tepee," Raven said. The twins watched, wide-
eyed, as Raven's fingers flashed, weaving the cord into
the shape of a tepee. Then, with a tug, he made the
tepee collapse. "Coyote worked too fast!" he said.
"He didn't tie the poles properly, and his tepee fell
down on him!" Everyone laughed, and the twins
squealed at the fun.

Raven leaned back on his elbows in the thick grass.
"I see you have a new horse, Little Sister," he said to
Kaya. "She's a pretty one."

"She's the prettiest horse in the whole herd!" Kaya
said with pride. Steps High wasn't large, only about
thirteen hands high. She had a black head and chest, a
white rump with black spots on it, and a white star on
her forehead. "She's fast, too," Kaya added. *That wasn't
boasting*, she thought—just saying what was true.

Fox Tail squatted beside her. He was a bothersome boy who could be rude. He always followed Raven, trying to impress the older boy. "Your horse looks skittish to me," he said to Kaya. "Why would your father give you a horse like that?"

"Toe-ta didn't choose my horse," Kaya said. "My horse chose me."

Fox Tail laughed and slapped his leg. "Your horse chose you? How?"

"One day I was riding by the herd with Toe-ta," Kaya said. "A filly kept nickering to me. So I whistled to her. She followed me. She came up to me and pushed her head against my leg. Toe-ta said that meant she wanted to be my horse. He worked with her so I could ride her."

"Is that a true story?" Fox Tail demanded.

"Ask my father if that's true," Kaya said.

"I believe you," Raven said. "But you say she's fast. Should I believe that, too?"

"I haven't raced her yet, but I've run her many times," Kaya said. "She glides over the ground like the shadow of an eagle."

Fox Tail jumped to his feet. "Like an eagle—big

talk!" he said. "Let's race our horses and see if yours flies like you claim she does!"

"Yes, let's race!" Raven got to his feet, too.

Kaya had an uneasy feeling. *I shouldn't have boasted about her speed,* she thought. *I've never raced her.* "My horse is tired now," she said hesitantly.

"She's not too tired for one short race," Fox Tail insisted. "Maybe your horse isn't so fast, after all."

Kaya felt her face grow hot. Her horse was as swift as the wind! She was sired by Toe-ta's fine stallion, Runner.

Kaya stood up. "Speaking Rain, could you take care of the twins for me?" she asked. "I know it's my job, but I want to race."

Speaking Rain was braiding strands of grass into bracelets for the little boys. "I'll try, but sometimes they play tricks on me."

"I'll only be gone a little while," Kaya assured her.

Kaya, Raven, and Fox Tail got on their horses and rode up to the raised plain at the end of the lake. Often people held celebrations and races here on the level ground, but today Kaya and the boys were alone.

Now that she'd decided to race, Kaya was eager to

begin. Steps High seemed eager, too. When Fox Tail's roan horse came close, Steps High arched her neck and flattened her ears. When Raven's chestnut horse passed her, she trotted faster.

Raven reined in his horse. "We'll start here. When I give the signal, we'll race until we pass that boulder at the far end of the field." He held his hand high. Then he brought it down and they were off!

The boys took the lead, stones spurting from under their horses' hooves. They lay low on their horses, their weight forward. They ran neck and neck.

Steps High bolted after them but swung out too wide. Kaya pressed her heels into Steps High's sides. Then she gave Steps High her head, and her horse sprang forward.

Kaya thrilled to feel her horse gather herself, lengthen out, and gallop flat out! She was running as she'd never run before. Her long strides were so smooth that she seemed to be floating, her hooves barely touching the earth. Her dark mane whipped Kaya's face. Grit stung Kaya's lips. She clung to her horse, barely aware that they'd caught the other horses until they passed them. She and Steps High were in the lead!

Then, suddenly, Steps High began to buck! She plunged, head down, heels high. Kaya grasped her mane and hung on. She bit her tongue and tasted blood. Steps High bucked again!

Raven spun his horse around. He was beside Steps High in an instant and grabbed the rein. He pulled the horse sharply to him, and, in the same motion, he halted his own horse. Steps High skidded to a standstill, foam lathering her neck. Kaya slid off.

Steps High's eyes were wild. For a moment she seemed never to have been tamed at all. Kaya's legs were shaking badly, but her first thought was to calm her horse. She began to stroke Steps High's trembling head and neck.

Fox Tail came galloping back. "I knew that horse was skittish!" he cried. "She just proved it!"

"She proved she's fast, too," Raven said.

Kaya wanted to thank Raven for coming to her aid, but her wounded pride was a knife in her chest. She could hardly get her breath. Leading her horse slowly to cool her down, Kaya silently walked away from the boys.

When Kaya had rubbed down Steps High, she

turned her horse out to graze. Then she started back through the woods, heading toward the river.

Her feelings were all tangled up like a nest of snakes. She was excited that Steps High had run so fast, but she was disappointed that her horse had broken her training. She was relieved that she hadn't been bucked off, but she wished the boys hadn't seen her lose control. She knew she shouldn't have boasted, but she also wished she could have made good on her boast and won the race.

When Kaya glanced up from nursing her hurt feelings, Fox Tail was coming down the trail toward her on foot. He stopped right in front of her. "You told us your horse chose you," he said with a smirk. "Would you choose her after the way she tried to buck you off today?"

"She's the best horse ever!" Kaya said. "She can run faster than your horse, and I can run faster than you, too. Want to race me right now?"

Fox Tail cocked his head. "The first one to the riverbank wins!" he cried. He turned and sprinted away down the path.

For a little while Kaya was right on his heels. Then

Fox Tail left the path, leapt over a fallen log, and took off through the woods. *He must know a shortcut*, Kaya thought. She followed him.

But she couldn't keep him in sight because he jagged in and out of shadows. Was that his dark head beyond the bushes? Now she was uncertain which way to go. She stopped to listen for the sound of the river as her guide.

She stood in a gloomy clearing surrounded by black willows. She listened for rushing water. There was only silence. No wind blew in the leaves, no flies buzzed. All she could hear was her heartbeat.

Then a twig snapped behind her. She whirled around. Did something just duck behind that tree? The shadows around her seemed to waver and sway. Was it the Stick People? Had they led her to this part of the woods?

Kaya held her breath. She knew the Stick People were cunning and crafty. They were strong, too. She'd heard they could carry off a baby and leave it a long way from its mother.

A flock of jays cawed—or was it the Stick People signaling to her? They seemed to be saying, "Forgot!

Forgot!" Kaya shivered. What had she forgotten?

Then she gasped. She'd forgotten her little brothers! Kaya should never have given her job to Speaking Rain. The little boys were four winters old, just the right age for mischief. Kaya must get back to them at once, before they got into danger.

She knew she must leave a gift for the Stick People in return for their help. They became angry with people who didn't treat them respectfully. She found rose hips in the bag she wore on her belt and placed them on the moss. Then she began running back the way she'd come.

Switchings!

aya ran along the riverbank, past women cleaning salmon and cutting the fish into thin strips. Auntie was laying the strips on racks to dry. She raised her hand in greeting when Kaya rushed by.

But Kaya kept going. She ran up to some girls setting up a little camp for their buckskin dolls. They'd made a travois with sticks and pieces of an old tule mat. A boy pretended to be their horse, pulling the travois. "Have you seen Speaking Rain and my brothers?" Kaya asked.

The children shook their heads, and Kaya ran on, desperate to find them.

The twins had never been like other little boys. They could understand each other without saying a word out loud. When they were born, the setting sun and the rising moon were both in the sky. Two lights in the sky and two babies who looked alike—they were special children. They could also be twice the trouble if they decided to play tricks.

Kaya ran through some brush and out onto the grassy bank where she'd last seen Speaking Rain with the boys. Speaking Rain crouched by a twisted pine tree, but the twins were nowhere in sight.

"Where are the boys?" Kaya called.

"I don't know," Speaking Rain said. "But I just found the toy I made for them." She held up a little hoop made of grass. "They got tired of my game and ran off. I've been calling them but they don't answer." Her cloudy eyes were wide with alarm. "Maybe they fell in the river!"

Kaya caught her breath. "Did you hear a splash?"

Speaking Rain shook her head. "But where could they be? Maybe a cougar chased them."

Cougars! Cougars sometimes went after small children. Kaya's heart raced, but she tried not to let Speaking Rain feel her alarm. "Come on, let's look for the boys. If they just ran off, they can't be far." She made herself sound confident, but she was frightened.

The boys could be hurt or lost. Oh, why hadn't she thought of them instead of herself?

Kaya looked around. Two trails led away from the riverbank. One turned upstream toward where the women worked. The other turned downstream. Dust-covered leaves hung low over that trail. The little boys probably would have been drawn to that leafy tunnel.

"Boys!" Kaya called. "Where are you?"

There was no answer.

"Follow me," Kaya said to Speaking Rain. "I'll look and you listen."

Speaking Rain took hold of Kaya's sleeve and walked right behind her down the trail.

"I see their footprints in the dust," Kaya said. She walked faster. "And here's where they left the trail and went under the bushes. They were crawling. We'll have to crawl, too. Stay close."

The girls got down on their hands and knees and inched forward. Leaves caught in their braids and brushed their cheeks. Kaya kept a lookout for the Stick People hiding in the shadows. Maybe they'd led the boys deeper into the woods.

A little farther on, the prints disappeared. Kaya

sat back on her heels. "I've lost their trail. Do you hear anything?"

Speaking Rain lifted her chin and frowned. "I hear the river. There's swift water there. If the boys fell in, they'd be swept away."

Kaya put her hand on Speaking Rain's shoulder. "Let's keep looking," she said. She began to search for prints again.

"I think we should get others to help us," Speaking Rain said. Then she pointed up. "Listen, I hear something up there!"

Kaya got to her feet so that she could see over the bushes. An old spruce tree loomed overhead. A cougar might be crouching in the branches! Or the boys. She'd been so busy following signs on the ground that she'd forgotten the twins could climb trees.

A spruce branch trembled. Two pairs of dark eyes gazed down at her from the green boughs. The boys were clinging to the trunk like raccoons. They were grinning.

Kaya was flooded with relief. She was also angry that the boys had scared her and Speaking Rain. "Come down right now!" she said.

The little boys crept down out of the tree in a shower of dry needles. When they reached the ground, they started to giggle.

Kaya took their hands and crouched to look into their eyes. "Don't laugh!" she said. "Running off isn't a game. Dangers are everywhere!"

"Yes, dangers are everywhere," a low voice said.

Startled, Kaya and Speaking Rain turned. Someone was coming through the woods behind them.

Hands parted the branches, and Auntie stepped through. Her face was stern. "When you ran by me I sensed trouble, so I followed you," she said. "Now I see I was right. I heard your mother tell you to look after your brothers. But you ran away from your responsibility."

Kaya felt her face redden. She bit her lips. Auntie's words made her ache with shame. "I'm sorry," she whispered.

"You should be sorry," Auntie said in a weary voice. "I must call Whipwoman to teach you a lesson."

As Kaya followed Auntie back to the camp, she kept a strong hold on her feelings so that they wouldn't show, but her eyes stung with unshed tears. She gazed at her feet when Auntie went to fetch Whipwoman, the respected elder selected to discipline children who misbehaved.

When Whipwoman arrived, she carried a bundle of switches. But it wasn't the switches that Kaya dreaded—it was the bad opinion of the other children. When one child misbehaved, *all* the children were disciplined. They learned that what one of them did affected all the rest.

"Come here, children!" Whipwoman called out. "Come here now!"

One by one, the children old enough to be switched came forward and lined up in front of Whipwoman. She laid her bundle of willow switches on the ground at her feet.

"Lie down on your stomachs and bare your legs," Whipwoman told them. She waited while everyone did as she said.

Kaya lay down, pulled her skirt up to her knees, and pressed her mouth to the back of her hand. She heard the switch hiss through the air and felt it sting her bare legs. She winced, but she didn't cry out or make a sound. Whipwoman moved on to Speaking

Rain, then to the next child. On and on she went until they'd all been given a switching.

As the children lay there, Whipwoman spoke to them slowly and firmly. "Kaya didn't watch out for her brothers. They ran off into the woods. They could have been injured. Enemies could have carried them away. A magpie that thinks only of itself would have given the boys better care than Kaya did! Nimíipuu always look out for each other. Our lives depend on it. Don't ever forget that, children. Now get up."

When Kaya lifted her head she caught sight of her parents and grandparents looking on. Their sad faces hurt her much more than the stings on her legs.

Fox Tail got to his knees near Kaya. He grimaced as he rubbed his legs. "Magpie!" he whispered to her. "I'm going to call you Magpie."

"Magpie! Magpie!" echoed the girl next to him.

Speaking Rain inched closer to Kaya and clasped her hand. "Don't mind them," Speaking Rain said. "It's all over now."

But it wasn't over. Kaya thought with alarm, *Magpie! Is Magpie going to be my nickname? Will they never let me forget this?*

◈

"These fish need to be prepared," Kaya's grandmother said to her. "Hold these sticks and give them to me as I need them."

It was later that day, and Aalah was preparing a welcome meal for Kaya's family. She knelt on a tule mat with several salmon in front of her. She was ready to cut up the salmon and place wooden skewers in the pieces so that they could be set by the fire to roast. Other women had dug deep pits to bake camas bulbs in. The delicious scent of roasting food filled the air.

Kaya was glad to be at her grandmother's side. Her head still buzzed with all the trouble she'd caused. Her problems had started with her beloved horse.

"I raced Steps High, but she tried to buck me off," Kaya confessed.

"Hmmm," Aalah muttered. She slid her knife up the belly of a salmon, cut off its head, took out its innards, and began to cut the rest into three long pieces. Her face shone with sweat from the heat of the fires. Her hands glistened with oil from the rich salmon.

One by one Kaya handed skewers to Aalah. "But I'm going to train her," Kaya said, thinking out loud. "Someday I'm going to be the very best horsewoman!" When she heard herself boast again, she bit her lip.

"Hmmm," Aalah muttered again. She laced a skewer through a large piece of fish. "I've lived a long time, and I've known many fine horsewomen. First they cared for their families. Then they trained their horses. You must think of others before yourself." She held out her hand for another skewer.

Kaya bowed her head at her grandmother's lecture. She felt a tear run down her nose.

"What's wrong?" Aalah asked. She laid aside a piece of fish and reached for the next one.

"Some children are calling me Magpie. They say I'm no more trustworthy than a thieving bird," Kaya said miserably.

"Nicknames!" Aalah said. "Have I ever told you the awful nickname I got when I was your age?" Her hands never stopped moving as she spoke.

Kaya shook her head. She couldn't imagine her grandmother doing anything to earn an awful nickname.

"Finger Cakes, that's what I was called," Aalah said. "Finger Cakes!"

Kaya couldn't help but smile. Women ground up kouse roots and shaped the mixture into loaves, or little finger cakes, to dry. Everyone liked dried kouse cakes. "That's a funny nickname," Kaya said. "Why did they call you that?"

Her grandmother picked up another large salmon. "My mother used to put a few finger cakes into my big brother's shoulder bag," she said. "If he got hungry when he was hunting, he'd chew on the finger cakes. I was jealous that he got extra pieces of my favorite food, so sometimes, when he wasn't looking, I'd steal some of his finger cakes. One day he caught me with my hand in his bag. From then on I was called Finger Cakes."

"Did they call you that for a long time?" Kaya asked.

"Yes, I was Finger Cakes for a long time," Aalah said. "Every time I heard that nickname, I remembered I'd been wrong to steal my brother's food. Every time I heard that nickname, I vowed I'd never again take what wasn't mine. It was a strict teacher, that nickname!"

"But you lost the nickname, didn't you?" Kaya said.
Her grandmother smiled. "Let me tell you something. Sometimes an old friend will call me Finger
Cakes just to tease me. After all these years that name
still pricks me like a thorn!" She put down her knife
and wiped her hands on the grass. "These salmon are
ready to roast now."

Kaya was still troubled. "Do you think I can lose
my nickname, Aalah?" she asked.

Her grandmother looked closely at Kaya. Her dark
eyes seemed to see right into Kaya's heart. "Listen to
me," Aalah said. "You're not a little girl any longer.
You're growing up. Soon you'll prepare to go on your
vision quest to seek your *wyakin*. Work hard to learn
your lessons so your nickname won't trouble you. Then
your thoughts will be clear when the time comes for
your vision quest." She pushed herself up from her
knees. "These fish need to be carried to the fire. Everyone is hungry."

Kaya's family gathered beside their tepee for their
evening meal. Aalah had laid several tule mats in a

row on the grass. The men took their places on one side
of the mats. The women set wooden bowls of salmon
and baked camas in the center and served the men.
Then the women sat down across from them.

Kaya's grandfather led them in giving thanks to
Hun-ya-wat, the Creator. *Kalutsa* held out his hands
over the feast. "Are you paying attention, children?"
he asked in his deep voice.

"Aa-heh!" Kaya said with the other children.

"Hun-ya-wat made this earth," Kalutsa said "He
made Nimíipuu and all people. He made all living
things on the earth. He made the water and placed
the fish in it. He made the sky and placed the birds
in it. He created food for all His creatures. We respect
and give thanks for His creations." After they all
sang a blessing, each one took a sip of water, which
sustains all life. Then they all took a tiny bite of
salmon, grateful that the fish had given themselves
to Nimíipuu for food. After that, Kalutsa motioned
for the rest of the food to be passed.

As Kaya ate, she glanced from time to time at the
others. She was surrounded by her grandparents,
parents, aunts and uncles, and all the children in her

family. She gazed at her father with his sharp cheekbones and broad shoulders. She looked at her mother
with her shining black hair and her straight brows.
Kaya felt how much she loved them all and how much
she needed them. She wanted to be worthy of their
trust, to be a girl no one would call Magpie ever again.

❀◆❀

"It is morning! We are alive! The sun is witness
to what we do today!" the camp crier called. He made
his way among the tepees to waken everyone and
announce the events of that day.

Kaya opened her eyes. Eetsa was already awake.
She'd brought a horn bowl of fresh water from the
river. Aalah was awake, too. She stood in the doorway
of the tepee and faced the east, where the dawn sky
glowed pink. With her eyes closed and her chin lifted,
Aalah sang a prayer of thanksgiving to Hun-ya-wat,
thanking Him for a good night's sleep and the new
day. Kaya silently joined Aalah's prayer. Morning
prayer songs were rising from all the tepees in the
camp.

The prayers over, Kaya stretched and yawned.

Beside her, Speaking Rain rolled onto her back and
reached for her folded dress. The twins were sitting on
the deerskin blanket they shared. They held out their
hands for the root cakes Brown Deer offered them.
Brown Deer had arisen before the camp crier passed
by, too. Although Kaya hoped to be as hard-working
and generous as her older sister, right now Kaya
wanted to stay curled up under her soft deerskin as
long as possible.

Aalah turned with a smile as if she guessed Kaya's
thought. "Come, girls, get up!" she said. "Roll up your
bedding. It's time to bathe in the river."

Every single morning of the year, in cold weather
as well as warm, all the children went into the river to
bathe. The cold water made them strong and healthy.
Grandmothers and Whipwoman watched the girls to
make sure they got clean.

This morning Kaya delighted in wading into the
quiet place at the river bend. A salmon tickled her toes
as she walked out on the pebbly bottom to where the
water reached her chest. As she splashed, the sun rose
over Mount Syringa and flooded light into the green
valley.

Rabbit, a girl older than Kaya, ducked underwater and came up next to her. She shook drops from her gleaming hair and gave Kaya a sly smile. "I didn't know magpies could swim," she whispered.

Kaya's cheeks burned. "I can swim, and faster than you!" she said.

"Will you peck if you catch me?" Rabbit laughed. With strong strokes she began to swim for shore.

Kaya swam after her. She could almost touch Rabbit's flashing heels, but she couldn't catch up to her. Kaya waded out of the river with her head bent.

"Magpie didn't win that race," Rabbit said with a grin.

That nickname stung like a hornet. *I let myself boast again!* Kaya realized with dismay as she dressed.

Kaya returned to their tepee, where she found her parents talking and laughing quietly together as Eetsa braided Toe-ta's thick black hair. When Eetsa had tied his braids together, Toe-ta beckoned to Kaya. "Let's go work with your horse," he said.

Toe-ta kept his best stallion, Runner, tethered on a long rope near the camp. He put a horsehair rope on Runner's lower jaw and mounted him bareback. He handed Kaya another rope bit and a long rope to carry.

Then he lifted her up behind him on the big horse, and they set out toward the herd.

Kaya loved to ride with her father. She leaned against his warm back. The smooth gait of Toe-ta's stallion rocked them gently. "Toe-ta, Steps High tried to buck me off yesterday," she said.

"I thought so," Toe-ta said. "I saw you walking her. If you hadn't had trouble, you'd have been riding."

"I know your horse would never buck you," Kaya said.

Toe-ta was quiet for a little while. "Have I told you about the first time my father put me on a horse?" he said.

"You've never told me that," Kaya said.

"I was a little boy, even younger than your brothers," Toe-ta said. "One day my father put me on the gentle old horse my grandmother rode. He told me to ride around the camp slowly. But after I went around slowly, I wanted to go faster. I kicked the horse as I'd seen my grandmother do. The horse bolted! My father chased us, yelling to me to turn the horse uphill to slow him. I looked for a soft spot and jumped off into the grass instead."

"Were you hurt, Toe-ta?" Kaya asked.

"I was sore all over!" he said. "Do you know why I told you that story today?"

"Why, Toe-ta?" Kaya asked.

"I want you to know that no one is born knowing how to ride," he said. "And you have to respect the horse you're riding. It takes a lot of work to learn what we need to know in this life."

Toe-ta swung Runner alongside a group of mares. Steps High was grazing with them.

"Whistle for your horse," he told Kaya. "She knows your whistle."

When Steps High heard Kaya's whistle, she pricked up her ears. As she came forward, Toe-ta tossed a rope around her neck and drew her close.

Each time Kaya saw Steps High, she marveled at her horse's beauty. Steps High was both graceful and strong, the muscles rippling under her skin.

Toe-ta got off his stallion and lifted Kaya down. As he approached Steps High, she tossed her small head and rolled her eyes. Toe-ta put the rope bit in her mouth, then grabbed a handful of mane as he swung onto her back. He held the rope reins firmly as he rode her away from the herd at a trot. Steps High pranced nervously, but she obeyed Toe-ta.

He drew the horse to a halt again by Kaya. "Now it's your turn," he said. "You're a strong rider. If you need me, I'm here to help."

Kaya swung up onto her horse. Toe-ta handed her the reins. But Kaya didn't urge Steps High forward.

"I won't push you too fast or too hard again," she whispered to her horse. "I want you to trust me."

Kaya pressed her knees to her horse's sides. She could feel a shiver run down her horse's back as Steps High began to walk. Steps High pushed against the bit as if she were thinking about running and bucking again, but she stayed at a walk until Kaya nudged her to trot. Kaya kept her horse gathered in and rode in slow circles until Toe-ta motioned for her to come back to him.

He took her horse's reins in one hand and stroked Steps High's neck. "Tawts," he said to Kaya. "That's just how you must ride her for a long time. Stay slow and stay in control. Work with her a little longer, then come back to camp." Toe-ta turned Runner and rode off.

As Kaya rode her horse in another circle, Fox Tail

rode up beside her. He'd been helping some older boys with the horses. His face was dusty, and his lips were dry. Herding was hard work in the hot sun. "Do you want to race again?" he asked Kaya.

"Toe-ta said I can't race my horse for a long time," Kaya said.

Fox Tail's grin was a wicked one. "I forgot that magpies don't race!" he cried. He kicked his horse and galloped away from her.

That nickname again! It gave Kaya a sick feeling in her stomach. She clenched her teeth as she circled Steps High back to the herd.

Courtship Dance

O ne morning, after many days of clear skies, dark clouds rolled over the mountains and rain pelted down. The tule reeds of the tepee coverings swelled with water and kept out the rain. The women turned from preparing food to work they could do inside the dry, cozy tepees until the storm passed.

Aalah took out the hemp cord and the beargrass she needed to weave some flat bags. She'd dyed the bear grass soft shades of red, green, and yellow. She gave some brown cord to Kaya, then started a bag for Speaking Rain to work on. Although Speaking Rain couldn't see, she could make fine cord and could weave by touch once Aalah set the first rows.

Eetsa and Brown Deer were mending moccasins for the twins, who napped on their deerskins. As he always did, Wing Feather slept with his hand tucked into his baby moccasin, which he cradled under his chin.

For a long time they worked in silence. Kaya liked the quiet tepee. The sound of rain falling on the tule mats soothed her. In fact, she wished she could stay inside their tepee, where no one called her Magpie, and never go out again.

Aalah touched Kaya's weaving to show her where her work was lumpy and uneven. "You're awake, but you're dreaming," Aalah said. "Will you tell me your dream?"

Kaya undid the line of weaving and started it over. She didn't want to admit how much that nickname still troubled her. "I was dreaming about my horse," she said.

"When I was a girl we didn't dream of horses," Aalah said with a smile. "When I was a girl we didn't even have horses. When we traveled we walked on our own two feet, and our strong dogs pulled our loads for us."

"You know about these things," Eetsa said respectfully. "But dogs couldn't pull the big loads that our horses do. And we couldn't travel as fast on foot as we can on horseback."

"But our scouts could run fast!" Aalah said. "The scouts who lived near the trail to enemy country ran as fast as the wind to warn us of danger." Aalah's fingers flew as she wove the bag. Already she'd finished a plain border and was adding a lovely pattern of triangles.

"It's true the scouts were swift," Eetsa said. "But no man runs as fast as a horse. No man can travel as far on foot as he can on horseback." She began sewing a new sole onto a moccasin with a length of sinew.

"Now the men ride far away, but often they don't come back for a long, long time," Aalah said. "Things were better in the old days."

"I can't imagine our warriors without their horses," Brown Deer said softly. "A warrior is so fierce on horseback! He fights so bravely!"

"Our men were brave warriors long before they ever heard of horses," Aalah said. "And because we have horses, our enemies make more raids on us."

"Aa-heh," Eetsa said. "You're right. But without his horse my husband wouldn't be such a good hunter. He

couldn't bring us so much meat. He always gives meat
to the old people, too."

"Horses are so beautiful!" Kaya chimed in.
"Especially the spotted ones, like Steps High!" She
imagined her horse running with her head held high
and her black tail streaming. Was it boasting to call
her beautiful?

Aalah reached for Kaya's bag and gently took it
from her. When Aalah put the tip of her finger through
a hole in a loose row, Kaya realized that she hadn't
made the weaving tight enough. She began to unravel
her work so that she could make it better.

"Aalah, you've often said we need horses for many
things," Brown Deer said.

Aalah sighed deeply. "I've said so and it's true,"
she said. "The old days are gone. We can't unravel
our lives and begin them again, as Kaya is doing with
her weaving." She put down her work and placed her
hands on her knees. "I want you to listen to me. I'm
going to tell you something."

Kaya and Speaking Rain laid down their weaving
at once. Eetsa and Brown Deer stopped sewing. When
Aalah spoke like that, she wanted their attention.

"I've lived a long time, and I remember many things," Aalah said. "Isn't that so?"

Eetsa and Brown Deer nodded.

"Aa-heh," Kaya and Speaking Rain said.

"One thing I remember is the time of terrible sickness," Aalah said. "Traders told us about strangers with pale, hairy faces who rode from far away to trade at the Big River. With the strangers on horses came a sickness of fevers and blisters, a sickness we'd never known before. My people never saw the strangers with pale faces, but their sickness came to us anyway. Many, many people sickened and died. The most powerful medicine man had no medicine to cure this new sickness."

Aalah was quiet for a while, gazing into space. Then she ran her hands across her cheeks. "You see these pockmarks on my face," she said. "I was one who got the sickness. My own mother died of it—I've told you that, too. These pockmarks remind me how few of us survived. They remind me that not just good things came into our lives with the horses. But the marks also remind me to be strong and help others."

Kaya looked at Aalah's solemn face. She knew

Aalah was thinking about the bad times in the past. Kaya was ashamed to be worrying about an unpleasant nickname when so much suffering had come to others. Would difficult times like the sickness come again to Nimíipuu?

"We've talked enough of that," Aalah said. "It's time to go back to work."

Kaya began her weaving again, making each twist of cord as firm and as tight as possible. When she grew up, she wanted to be a wise, strong woman like Aalah.

❈◆❈

"The men are getting out the drums again!" Speaking Rain said. "Soon they'll start singing. Listen!"

Kaya listened. From across the camp came the first drumbeats. Every evening, drumming, songs, and laughter filled the air. In the middle of the camp, Toe-ta and some other men were playing the stick game, joking and shouting as they made their guesses. The women watched and chatted with their friends. The children chased each other and played games. Soon there would be dancing, too, until it was time for the men to light fires along the riverbank and begin their night fishing. Kaya loved being part of so much excitement.

In their tepee, Kaya watched Brown Deer dress for the courtship dance. Brown Deer put on her best dress, decorated with porcupine quills and elk teeth. She tied on her wide belt and hung a small woven bag from it. She smoothed the ankle flaps of her moccasins and tied them neatly.

"Your dress is so beautiful!" Kaya exclaimed.

Speaking Rain folded her arms and grinned up at her older sister. "Tell us, who do you want to dance with tonight?"

"I don't know," Brown Deer said with a shrug and the flicker of a smile.

As Brown Deer hurried to join the others, Kaya thought her big sister was the prettiest girl in the whole village.

Kaya and Speaking Rain followed her out of the tepee. In the light of the rising moon, the twins were dancing, hopping about and bobbing their heads like quail. Wing Feather beat two sticks together. Sparrow spun around until he was dizzy and fell to his knees.

Kaya was too young to join the courtship dance,
but the drumbeats and singing made her want to whirl
around and around like Sparrow. They made her want
to beat the rhythm like Wing Feather. As Kaya listened,
she practiced dancing by taking small steps, moving in
place. Who could resist the drums!

On one side of the clearing, the older girls began
to form a circle. The older boys formed a circle around
the girls for the courtship dance. In this dance a boy
tried to dance beside the girl he liked best. If a girl let
him stay by her side, that meant she liked him best, too.
Most families decided who would marry whom, but
some paid attention to the choices of the dancers in the
courtship dance.

"Brown Deer's dancing near us," Kaya whispered to
Speaking Rain.

"Is she looking at any special boy?" Speaking Rain
asked.

"She looks at all the boys but one," Kaya said.
"She never looks at Cut Cheek."

Cut Cheek was slim and strong. He was a good
hunter and a good dancer, too. The scar on his cheek
only made him better-looking, Kaya thought. She'd

often seen him glance at Brown Deer as he danced, but Brown Deer never returned his gaze.

"When Cut Cheek comes near, Brown Deer looks at her moccasins," Kaya said. "I don't think she likes him at all."

Speaking Rain giggled. "Kaya, you're foolish!" she said. "If Brown Deer can't bring herself to look at Cut Cheek, that means she really likes him."

"But how will he know she likes him if she never looks at him?" Kaya wondered.

"He'll know!" Speaking Rain said.

All the young men and women were in the circle now. When the drumbeats changed, the boys and girls danced slowly forward toward each other. The long fringes on the girls' dresses rippled and swung as the girls moved. The drums seemed to be saying, *Come dance with me! Dance with me!* With exciting music like this, how could the dancers keep their steps so steady and even?

"Where's Cut Cheek dancing?" Speaking Rain asked.

"He's on the other side of the circle," Kaya said. "I don't think he'll be able to get near Brown Deer."

The dancers moved close to each other, then away, then close again. The next time they were close, a boy eased himself out of his line and placed a stick on a girl's right shoulder. She kept the stick on her shoulder and made room for him by her side. Now they danced as a couple.

The dancers moved toward each other again. As they advanced, Cut Cheek managed to move past the boy next to him. Now he was almost in front of Brown Deer. She held her chin high and looked straight ahead. She made the fringe on her dress snap with each graceful step.

"What's happening now?" Speaking Rain asked impatiently.

"Cut Cheek keeps moving closer to Brown Deer," Kaya said.

Again the dancers moved forward. The boy called Jumps Back moved opposite Brown Deer. He was short, with broad shoulders. Although he often liked to tease the girls, now he looked very serious. When Brown Deer danced close to him, Jumps Back stepped beside her and placed his stick on her shoulder. With a shrug, she knocked the stick off. Jumps Back bent to pick up his stick, and Cut Cheek moved into his place. Now he was opposite Brown Deer.

"Brown Deer just turned down Jumps Back," Kaya told Speaking Rain. "Cut Cheek is right in front of her. But she's looking past him as if she doesn't even know he's there."

"Oh, she knows he's there!" Speaking Rain giggled.

The next time the dancers were close, Cut Cheek left the boys' line. His dark face was gleaming. He stepped next to Brown Deer and placed his stick on her shoulder. Blushing, she took a deep breath as if she were about to dive into deep water. She let his stick stay on her shoulder, and they danced now side by side.

"She chose Cut Cheek!" Kaya said. "She didn't hesitate for a moment!"

The run of salmon up the river was coming to an end. Many, many salmon had given themselves to Nimíipuu. The women had packed the dried salmon into large, woven bags and parfleches made of raw-hide. Now they were packing up their belongings as well. Soon the women would roll up the tule mat

coverings of the tepees and take down the tepee poles.
They would put everything they owned on their
horses and the travois and set out. It was time to move
higher into the mountains so that the women could
pick huckleberries and the men could hunt for elk and
deer. Kaya and her family would be part of the group
traveling back to Salmon River Country.

Aalah called Kaya to her. She looked worried.
"I think I left my knife where we were working
yesterday," Aalah said.

"I'll go look carefully," Kaya said.

Kaya already had a rope bit on Steps High. She'd
been riding her horse every day, keeping her tightly
reined in and held to a trot. Steps High hadn't once
tried to buck off Kaya. But Kaya hadn't yet asked
Toe-ta if it was safe to run her horse again.

"May I come with you, Kaya?" Speaking Rain
asked. Kaya gave Speaking Rain her hand and pulled
her sister up onto the horse to sit behind her. Riding
bareback, they trotted away from the camp.

At the river, they passed Toe-ta and a few other
men fishing for the last of the salmon. Fox Tail and
some other boys were helping.

Toe-ta stood on the bank with his back to the sun.
He had placed a large white stone in the current where
the river was shallow. When a fish swam between the
white stone and Toe-ta, he could see its outline and
spear it.

Downstream, where the river was deeper, Aalah
had been cleaning fish on the bank the day before.
Kaya reined in Steps High. "I'll start searching a little
way down the path and make my way back to you,"
Kaya told Speaking Rain. "Wait here to mark where
I started my search." Speaking Rain slipped off Steps
High. As Kaya rode on down the path, she looked for
her grandmother's knife.

Steps High was tense and skittish. She shied at a
garter snake crossing the path, but Kaya steadied her.
When Steps High shied a second time, Kaya reined
her in. "What's the matter, girl?" Kaya asked. "What's
spooking you?" Steps High snorted and pawed the
ground.

Kaya shaded her eyes and looked back to where
Speaking Rain had been waiting. Speaking Rain was
cautiously making her way through the elderberry
bushes that grew along the riverbank. She couldn't

know there was a steep bank on the other side of the bushes. "Stop, Speaking Rain!" Kaya called. She turned Steps High and started back.

Speaking Rain didn't seem to hear Kaya's call. Were Stick People leading her astray? She kept going. "Stop! Don't take another step!" Kaya cried.

Now Speaking Rain heard Kaya's cry. She stopped and turned. As she did, a piece of the bank crumbled beneath her feet. Speaking Rain fell backward. In a shower of stones, she tumbled into the swift river!

Rescued from
the River

aya drove Steps High forward. She jumped her over the bushes and reined her in sharply, her hooves plowing the ground. Speaking Rain was struggling in deep water, trying to swim toward shore. As she thrashed, a branch plunged down in the swift current and hit her. She went under. When she came up again, she was being pulled downstream in the powerful surge of the river.

Fear struck through Kaya like a lightning flash. If Speaking Rain wasn't pulled from the river, she'd drown. If Kaya tried to swim after her, they could both drown. To save Speaking Rain, Kaya's only hope was to run her horse along the bank, try to get ahead of Speaking Rain, and ride into the river to catch her.

Kaya gave her horse her head, then kicked her. Steps High burst forward. In a few strides she was at a full gallop. Kaya leaned low over her neck, clasping her horse with her knees. What if another piece of riverbank gave way? What if her horse bucked? Steps High lengthened out and tore around the next bend, then the next. She seemed as swift as a hawk diving from the sky! Now they were ahead of Speaking Rain, who flailed in the churning river. From here, Kaya had to get her horse into the water and then swim upstream to meet Speaking Rain as she was swept down.

Would Steps High obey Kaya's command to swim? Kaya dug her heels into her horse's sides and again urged her forward. Steps High crossed the beach but paused at the edge of the water. "Come on, girl!" Kaya said, giving her another kick. Then Kaya felt Steps High become one with her again. The horse moved out into the icy current until she was swimming.

Kaya angled her horse upstream. She held tightly to Steps High's mane to keep her balance against the swirling currents. She'd have to catch Speaking Rain as soon as she came within reach, or else Speaking Rain would be swept under the horse's sharp hooves. In another moment, Speaking Rain was upon her. Kaya reached and grasped, caught her arm—she had her! She pulled and dragged Speaking Rain over her horse's withers. Holding Speaking Rain tightly, Kaya turned her horse downstream. She felt Steps High gather herself.

The horse's strokes evened out as she calmed. But Speaking Rain was limp against Kaya. Was she breathing? Kaya headed Steps High toward shore.

In a few more strokes, her horse's hooves touched bottom. Steps High's head came up, and she climbed onto the sandy beach. She shook her head and pranced a step or two as if she knew she'd done something to be proud of.

Kaya slid off her horse and caught Speaking Rain as her sister slipped down into her arms. Speaking Rain lifted her head, moaned, and began to cough up water. "You're safe, Speaking Rain!" Kaya said against her drenched head. "You're safe!"

Toe-ta appeared on the bank above them. He was followed by the other fishermen and by Fox Tail. Toe-ta leaped down onto the sand. He took Speaking Rain into his arms, bent her forward, and slapped her back with his cupped hand to force more water from her.

Kaya's teeth were chattering. "Speaking Rain, can you get your breath?" she asked.

"Aa-heh," Speaking Rain gasped.

"I heard you shout, and I ran," Toe-ta said. "I saw what happened. You did well, Kaya. Your horse did well, too."

"Steps High knew Speaking Rain needed us," Kaya said. "She did everything I asked of her."

"She did what you asked because she trusts you," Toe-ta said. "You've earned her trust, remember that."

Fox Tail crouched on the bank. Was that a look of admiration in his eyes? "You told me you couldn't race," he said. "But you were racing like wildfire, Kaya."

"Kaya wasn't racing to be the fastest," Toe-ta corrected him. "She was racing to save Speaking Rain's life."

Toe-ta's words lifted Kaya's heart. He knew she hadn't acted for herself, but for Speaking Rain. And Fox Tail had called her Kaya, not Magpie!

Kaya closed her eyes, pressed her face against Steps High's warm, wet neck, and felt the powerful pulse beating there. "*Katsee-yow-yow*, my horse!" she

whispered gratefully. Then she held the bridle so that
Toe-ta could lift Speaking Rain onto Steps High's back
and they could take her back to camp.

❄◆❄

The horses needed fresh grass before they could
begin the journey higher into the mountains. Kaya
rode with Raven, Fox Tail, and some older boys and
girls to herd the horses to new pasture. As Kaya rode,
she gazed up at a tall peak. She knew the story of how
the mountain came to be. An old chief had a vision.
His vision told him that men with pale faces would
come to steal the shining rocks scattered here. To
protect their shining rocks, the people gathered them
into a pile and built the mountain over them to hide
them. Their treasure was saved because of the old
chief's vision.

Kaya thought that if she'd lived in those days,
she'd have helped build the mountain over the shining
rocks. After all, her name—*Kaya'aton'my'*—meant
"she who arranges rocks." Her mother gave her that
name because the first thing she saw after Kaya's birth
was a woman arranging rocks to heat a sweat lodge.

Will one of us be given a vision someday? Kaya
wondered. *Will I?*

She knew that one day soon, like all the other boys
and girls, she would go on her vision quest. *Will I be
ready when that time comes?* she thought.

When she went into the mountains on her quest,
Kaya would seek her wyakin. If her wyakin came to
her, she could also receive special powers. Would the
hawk give her the ability to see far? Would the canyon
wren give her the power to defend her family, the way
the wren drives off rattlesnakes? *What creature will my
wyakin be?* Kaya wondered. She hoped it would give
her powers and a vision to help Nimíipuu, like the old
chief in the story.

Fox Tail rode past, his big roan kicking up a cloud
of dust. *Fox Tail's too much of a rascal to become a leader
of our people,* Kaya thought. But maybe the old chief,
whose vision saved the shining mountain, had once
been a bothersome boy like Fox Tail.

Kaya reminded herself to think of the work of the
day and to do her job well. A frisky young stallion
bolted out of the herd and passed behind Kaya and
her horse. Immediately, she swung Steps High around,

dug in her heels, and galloped after the runaway. Steps High knew her job, too. In a burst of speed, she caught up to the frisky horse and drove him back into the herd again. "Tawts!" Kaya said, and patted Steps High's shoulder. "Tawts, my beautiful horse!"

Taken Captive!

aya dug her fists into the sides of her waist and stretched. Her back was sore from bending over to pick huckleberries. Since first light, she and the other girls had moved along the hillside, plucking ripe berries from the bushes and dropping them into the baskets they wore at their waists. Now the sun was high overhead. It was time to sort and dry the berries they'd picked in the cooler hours. Kaya thought dried berries were good, but ripe ones were a feast. When she thought no one was looking, she sneaked a handful for herself.

"Look, Magpie's stealing berries!" Little Fawn cried. "If she eats too many now, we won't have enough when winter comes!" She gave Kaya a teasing grin.

Kaya winced. Not a single day went by without someone calling her by her awful nickname—Magpie.

Each time Kaya heard that name, it stung like Whip-woman's switch!

It was now late summer, and Kaya was back in Salmon River Country, where her family had joined her mother's band of Nimíipuu. They had traveled upstream and set up camp to pick berries in the higher country. Her father and many of the other men had gone even farther into the mountains to scout the deer and elk trails. It was time for the hunt. Soon the men would bring back as much game as they could so that everyone would have plenty of meat for the winter. With the dried meat, fish, and berries, there would be good provisions for the cold season to come.

Kaya untied the basket from her belt and spread leaves over the berries to keep them from falling out of the basket. She set her basket with those her mother and her big sister, Brown Deer, had filled. All the women and girls had been berry picking. Even the youngest girls wore little baskets—though they were allowed to eat more berries than they saved.

Kaya's grandmother was loading baskets onto her horse. *Kautsa* glanced over her shoulder at Kaya, then nodded at a little girl with her tiny basket. "Remember

when you were that young?" she asked Kaya.
"Remember how you'd run to give me the first few
berries you picked?"

Kaya smiled, glad to be reminded of those happy
days. "I remember you always praised me for my
berries," she said. "You said I'd be a good picker
one day."

"And you are!" Kautsa said. She hung the last bags
onto her saddle, then patted her horse. Leading it, she
began to walk with the others down to the tepees set
in the meadow near the stream.

Kaya walked alongside Kautsa, matching her
strides to her grandmother's long ones. Heat rose from
the stony path and shimmered around her legs. "The
sun's hot, isn't it?" she said.

"Aa-heh!" Kautsa agreed. "The day is hot and our
work is hard. But we need to pick berries so we won't
go hungry this winter."

Kaya studied the thick groves of lodgepole pines
that ringed the meadow below. "Could Speaking
Rain and I sleep outside the tepee tonight?" she asked.
"I think we'd be cooler in the meadow."

"We'll be cool enough inside," Kautsa said. "I

want you two near me. With many of our men away, we'll be safer if we stay close together. The boys are keeping the herd close by, too. Look, there's your horse with the others."

Kaya shaded her eyes. She quickly identified Steps High by the star on her forehead. Kaya's horse was grazing at the edge of the herd with some mares and their foals. Perhaps Steps High sensed Kaya's approach, for she lifted her head and whinnied.

Kautsa halted her horse. She picked some large leaves from a thimbleberry plant beside the trail, then sprinkled a pinch of dried roots on the earth in thanks for what she'd taken. She used the leaves to wipe sweat from Kaya's forehead and then to dry her own face. "Go sit in the shade with Speaking Rain for a little while," she said. "The heat has tired you."

Kaya found Speaking Rain sitting under a pine tree. Because Speaking Rain was blind, she'd stayed in the camp with the elderly women and men. She was weaving a beargrass basket that Kautsa had begun for her.

"I brought you some huckleberries, Little Sister," Kaya said. She placed a handful of berries into

Speaking Rain's outstretched hands. Kaya sat beside
Speaking Rain in the shade of the pine tree. "Our dogs
chased two black bears out of the berry bushes this
morning," Kaya said.

"Everyone wants these berries," Speaking Rain said.
She ate hers one by one, making them last as long as
possible. As she munched, she tipped her head toward
Kaya. "Why do you sound so sad?"

Kaya knew she couldn't hide anything from
Speaking Rain. Maybe because Speaking Rain couldn't
see, she heard everything sharply. "Little Fawn caught
me sneaking huckleberries," Kaya admitted with a
sigh. "She called me Magpie again."

"I hope that nickname will fade soon," Speaking
Rain said. Again she cocked her head, listening.
"Isn't that your horse whinnying to you? Go to her.
Nicknames don't mean a thing to a horse!"

Gratefully, Kaya squeezed Speaking Rain's hand—
Speaking Rain always understood her.

As Kaya walked toward the herd, she whistled
her horse to her side. Steps High rubbed her head
against Kaya's shoulder. Her horse's muzzle was as
soft as the finest buckskin. "Hello, beautiful one!"

Kaya whispered against the horse's sleek neck. It always comforted Kaya to stroke her horse.

As Steps High nuzzled her, Kaya glanced back at
the clearing where women spread the berries on tule
mats to dry in the sun. She saw her two little brothers
bouncing on a crooked cedar tree, pretending to ride
a horse. Nearby, little girls played with their buckskin
dolls. Dogs lolled beside the tepees, their tongues out.
In the wide meadow, boys rode herd on the horses.
Thin clouds drifted toward the Bitterroot Mountains
in the east. *Stay close to be safe*, Kautsa had reminded
her. Kautsa was wise in these things, and Kaya had
heard that warning all her life. But right now, this quiet
valley seemed the safest place she could imagine.

"Listen!" Kautsa said in a low voice. "The dogs are
growling! Wake up!"

Kaya tried to waken in the deep of night. She heard
Kautsa's sharp command, but sleep was like a hand
pushing her down. Nearby, some dogs growled, then
began to bark fiercely. Kaya sat up and rubbed her eyes.
What was wrong?

Her mother peeked out the door of the dark tepee, then ducked back inside. "Strangers in our camp!" Eetsa said. "Get dressed! Quick! Enemies!"

Enemies! Enemies in their camp! The warning was a jolt of lightning—swiftly Kaya was on her feet. Her heart pounding, she struggled into her dress. Kautsa, Brown Deer, and Speaking Rain were doing the same. They all tugged on their moccasins and crept out of the tepee. Kautsa pushed Speaking Rain and the twin boys ahead of her. Brown Deer picked up one of the little boys. Eetsa picked up the other one. "Follow me!" Eetsa whispered. "Kaya, take Speaking Rain to the woods! We'll hide there!" Crouching, Eetsa ran for the trees, Brown Deer and Kautsa right on her heels.

The moon was rising above the trees bordering the clearing. Kaya could see women, children, and old people hurrying from the tepees for safety in the woods. Some men ran toward the edge of the camp where dark figures ducked between the horses tethered there. Raiders! Enemy raiders! They'd slipped into camp hoping to make off with the best horses, but the dogs had given them away.

Kaya's mouth was dry with alarm. She clasped

Speaking Rain's hand tightly. But instead of following Eetsa into the woods, as she'd been told, she went in the direction of the herd. Where was Steps High? Would raiders try to steal her horse?

Kaya saw the woman named Swan Circling head toward the horses, too. A raider was about to cut the rawhide line that tethered her fine horse. Swan Circling had as much courage as any warrior. She stabbed at the raider with her digging stick. She knocked him away from her horse, which reared and whinnied in panic.

The raider leaped onto the back of another horse he'd already cut loose. With a fierce cry, he swung the horse around and galloped straight through camp, coming right at Kaya and Speaking Rain!

With a gasp of fear, Kaya tried to run out of his way, pulling Speaking Rain behind her. Too late! Kaya threw herself onto her stomach, dragging Speaking Rain down with her. The raider jumped his horse over them and plunged on.

Kaya struggled to her knees. Now other raiders raced through the camp toward the herd. They lay low on their horses, trying to stampede the herd so no one could ride after them. The horses snorted and screamed with alarm. A few broke away. Was Steps High with them? Kaya whirled around. Nimíipuu men with bows and arrows were running to cut off the raiders.

Arrows hissed by. Kaya clasped Speaking Rain's hand again and ran for the safety of the woods. A horse brushed against her, almost knocking her down. She felt someone seize her hair, then grasp her arm. Speaking Rain's hand was yanked from hers. A raider swung Kaya roughly behind him onto his horse. She sank her teeth into his arm, but he broke her hold with a slap.

Kaya looked back for Speaking Rain. Another raider was dragging her onto his horse. "Speaking Rain!" Kaya cried, but her cry was lost in the tumult. The raiders raced after the herd, which ran full out now. The Nimíipuu men gave chase on foot, but they were quickly outdistanced.

Terrified, Kaya clung to the raider's back. The herd was thundering down the valley, the raiders in the rear. The night was filled with boiling dust. Hoofbeats shook the ground and echoed in Kaya's chest. She caught a glimpse of Steps High running with the others. Her horse had been stolen by the enemies. She was their captive, too, and so was Speaking Rain. And it was Kaya's fault!

All that night, and on through the next day and night, the raiders ran the stolen horses eastward. When their mounts tired, they paused only briefly before jumping onto fresh horses and going on. Kaya knew they wanted to get out of Nimíipuu country before they were caught.

Because the raiders didn't rest, Kaya and Speaking Rain couldn't rest, either. The mountains and the valleys below went by in a blur. In her fatigue, Kaya sometimes thought she saw a blue lake in the sky. Sometimes she thought the distant, rolling hills were huge buffalo. And sometimes she did fall asleep, her head bumping the raider's back. He slapped her legs to waken her. She thought, then, about jumping off the running horse, but she knew she'd be injured or killed on the narrow, stony trail. *Maybe it would be better to die than to be a captive,* Kaya thought. But she couldn't abandon Speaking Rain.

When the sun was high overhead, the raiders finally stopped to rest. They left a scout to guard their trail and took the herd to a grassy spot by a little lake

where the horses could feed and drink. Kaya saw
Steps High standing by the water with the other
foam-flecked horses. Their heads were down, and
their chests heaved from the punishing journey.
How she wished she could go to her horse!

When the raiders gathered to share dried meat,
Kaya got a better look at them. They were young,
bold, and proud of themselves for stealing so many
fine horses. She thought they spoke the language of
enemies from Buffalo Country. Though Kaya couldn't
understand their words, she knew that they boasted of
their success. Perhaps they were proud, too, that they
had driven the herd all the way through Nimíipuu
country to the northern trail through the Bitterroot
Mountains.

The raider who'd seized Speaking Rain offered her
some of the buffalo meat. When she didn't respond, he
waved his hand in front of her eyes, then made a noise
of disgust. Kaya knew he was angry that the girl he'd
captured for a slave was blind. He pushed her down
beside Kaya and stalked back to the circle of men.
Kaya held her close.

Speaking Rain leaned against Kaya's shoulder.

"Where are we?" she whispered.

"Somewhere on the trail to Buffalo Country," Kaya whispered back. She put some of the food she'd been given into Speaking Rain's hand.

"What will happen to us?" Speaking Rain's voice quavered.

Though Kaya trembled with fatigue, she kept her voice steady. "Don't you remember what happened when enemies from the south stole some of our horses? Our father and the other warriors got ready for a raid. As the drummers beat the drums, all the women sang songs to send off our warriors with courage. Our warriors followed the enemies over the mountains and brought back all our horses! Our warriors will make a raid on these men, too. They'll take you and me back home with them. And they'll take back all of our horses, as well."

"Are you sure?" Speaking Rain murmured.

"Aa-heh!" Kaya whispered. "I'm sure."

But, in her heart, Kaya was far from certain. They'd traveled a long way over the mountains already. Toe-ta and the other men might not have returned to the berry-picking camp yet. When they did, the raiders might have already left the mountains and hidden themselves securely in the country to the east. What would happen to Kaya and Speaking Rain—and Steps High—then?

Kaya squeezed Speaking Rain's hand. "We have to be strong, Little Sister."

"Aa-heh," Speaking Rain agreed. "We'll be strong."

One of the raiders motioned for the girls to lie down. He tied Kaya's leg to Speaking Rain's with a length of rawhide so they couldn't run away. Lying huddled together, they softly prayed to Hun-ya-wat, asking for strength. Kaya was exhausted, but her head buzzed with fears. "I'm afraid to sleep," she whispered to Speaking Rain.

"Me, too," Speaking Rain whispered back. She put her cheek against Kaya's shoulder. "Remember the lullaby that Kautsa used to sing to us?"

Kaya nodded. Then, to her surprise, Speaking Rain began to sing gently, "*Ha no nee, ha no nee.* She's my precious one, my own dear little precious one."

Lulled by Speaking Rain's gentle voice, Kaya slept.

Slaves of the Enemy

T he raiders moved the herd eastward over the Buffalo Trail as quickly as they could. As they rode, Kaya caught glimpses of the Lochsa River in the valley, but the trail stayed on the top of the ridge. The going was easier up here than in the wooded gullies filled with windfall trees.

Kaya had been on this trail before. It was an old, old pathway made long before Nimíipuu had horses. In some places it split and braided together again where travelers had walked around fallen trees or boulders. In other places it was only a narrow ledge hugging a cliff. Kaya watched the horses carefully when they came to the dangerous ledges. Surely the raiders were pushing them too fast along this bad part of the trail. A horse that lost its footing would fall down the rocky slope and perhaps be killed.

The gentle old pack horse that belonged to Kautsa often stumbled in fatigue. Kaya kept her eye on the old horse, hoping he could keep up. But on a curving ledge, he slipped on the loose rocks. Kaya held back a cry as the old horse tumbled down the bluff in a shower of stones and lay still at the bottom. Wouldn't the raiders slow the other horses now? But no, they only pushed them faster. Kaya kept her gaze on Steps High and prayed that her horse would keep her footing. *Be strong!* she urged Steps High—and herself. Where were the enemies taking them?

Each night at last light, they camped in open glades where the horses could graze. A raider back-scouted the trail to see if they were followed. Kaya hoped that Toe-ta and other men were coming behind and would overpower the raiders. She thought that young men from Buffalo Country were no match for Nimíipuu men! But when the scout returned and the raiders continued on without rushing, Kaya knew no one was behind them.

At the highest point on the pass, Kaya gazed back at the mountains that loomed between her and her home country. Her courage sank low. She told herself

that Hun-ya-wat had made the sky above her and the
earth beneath her. *I am in His home no matter where I go,*
she thought. Still, fear was a bitter taste in her mouth as
they moved farther from her people.

Each night the raiders tied Kaya's leg to Speaking
Rain's. At first light, the raiders untied them and sent
Kaya to gather heavy loads of wood for the fire. They
fed Kaya and Speaking Rain only the scraps from
their meals. Kaya felt like the starving dogs that sometimes appeared at camp out of nowhere, cringing and
groveling for a bite of food. She vowed that if she ever
got back to her people again, she would never chase off
those desperate, sad-eyed dogs.

When they passed some hot springs, where
steaming water spouted from the rocks, the trail ran
down the east side of the mountains. In another day
they'd reached the broad river valley below. Kaya
remembered passing this way with her family when
they went to hunt buffalo on the plains beyond.
Then, this country had seemed full of promise and
adventure. Now, it seemed strange and menacing. A
wide, swift river flowed north, down the valley. If the
raiders crossed the river, they'd be well on their way to

their home country. How would she and her sister get home from so far away?

In this valley, the raiders moved the horses at night to avoid being seen. Shortly after first light they came to a small buffalo-hunting camp of their people, hidden in a canyon. The hide-covered tepees were decorated with animals and birds painted in brilliant colors, so different from the brown tule mat tepees of Kaya's people. As the raiders approached the camp, the hunters and the women gathered to greet them.

The raiders rode proudly through the camp, displaying the horses—and the girls—they'd stolen. Though Kaya wouldn't let her feelings show, she was sick to see the raiders praised and honored. She winced when the men looked over the horses and stroked the ones they liked best, Steps High among them. How she hated to have enemy hands on her horse!

All the men and women in the camp were pleased and smiling, except one dirty boy with a sullen face who stared grimly at Kaya. It came to her that the angry-looking boy was a slave, too, and that soon she and Speaking Rain would look as tired and bitter as he.

Kaya stared at her feet when the women came to

inspect her and Speaking Rain. The women pinched
the girls' arms to feel their muscles, then shook their
heads and talked among themselves. They didn't
sound pleased.

Kaya and Speaking Rain were dirty and their hair
was tangled. They were used to bathing in the cold
river and cleansing themselves in the heat of the sweat
lodge every single day. Since they'd been captured,
they hadn't been able to wash.

When the women saw Speaking Rain's cloudy
eyes, they frowned and spoke angrily to the raiders.
Were they saying that a blind slave was nothing more
than another belly to feed? Would they decide that
Speaking Rain was no use to them and abandon her
here, so far from Salmon River Country? But one raider
took Speaking Rain's arm and led her to a young
mother with a baby. He said something that caused the
mother to look more kindly at Speaking Rain. Kaya
guessed he'd told the mother that the blind girl wasn't
entirely useless—she could sing lullabies and could
help tend the baby while the mother worked. Kaya
hoped they'd soon realize what a skilled cord maker
and weaver Speaking Rain was, too.

One of the older women, with gray hair and a
lined face, led Kaya to her tepee. Bold designs of
otters were painted on the tepee in bright yellow and
red. Kaya thought of the old woman as Otter Woman.
She sat Kaya down and gave her buffalo meat to eat.
When Kaya had eaten, the woman took Kaya to where
other women were cleaning hides. She handed Kaya
a sharp-edged rib bone and made a scraping motion.
She wanted Kaya to scrape the fat and meat from a
hide that was staked to the ground.

Kaya had often helped Kautsa clean hides. She
knelt by the buffalo hide and began to scrape at it with
the rib bone. Otter Woman watched her work for a
little while, then nodded in satisfaction. Kaya scraped
even harder, until her shoulders ached and her arms
were sore—she vowed to work twice as hard in order
to make up for Speaking Rain. Somehow she must
protect her sister.

When night came, Otter Woman led Kaya and
Speaking Rain into her tepee. She spread hides for
them beside her sleeping place and motioned for them
to lie down. Taking a thick rawhide thong, she tied it
around Kaya's ankle and then around her own. She

made the knots tight so Kaya couldn't untie the thong
and run away. She didn't bother to tie up Speaking
Rain—a blind girl wouldn't try to escape.

Speaking Rain pressed against Kaya's side.
"Be strong," Kaya whispered to her.

Otter Woman gave her a sharp pinch that meant,
Hush! Go to sleep!

Kaya clenched her teeth and vowed she would not
cry, not even in the dark. But how could she sleep when
her heart was aching so badly? She and Speaking Rain
were slaves—they might never see their people again.

At first light, Kaya was sent to gather firewood.
She watched the hunters ride away from camp to hunt
buffalo in the valley. Later in the day, when the men
returned with the buffalo they had killed, they gave the
meat and hides to the women. Otter Woman set Kaya
to work and led Speaking Rain to sing to the baby.

All day the women worked, cutting up the meat
and hanging the strips on poles to dry. They scraped
and tanned the hides, wasting nothing. Kaya's arms
and back ached from the hard work of scraping. When
she grew dizzy from the sun and weary from the work,
she told herself to be strong for Speaking Rain.

Black-and-white magpies swooped over the drying meat, stealing bits for themselves. Magpie— Kaya's nickname. She had tried to be more responsible, but then she'd disobeyed Eetsa's order to run for safety in the woods.

That mistake had put her and Speaking Rain into captivity. *Maybe I deserve that nickname, after all*, Kaya thought miserably. She picked up a magpie feather and put it in the bag on her belt, a reminder that she *must* think of others before herself.

From where Kaya worked, she often caught glimpses of Steps High grazing with the other horses. If only she could get to her horse, touch her, stroke her! Kaya watched for a chance to approach the herd, but the boys who tended the horses never seemed to leave them.

One evening, when the sun blazed on the horizon, Kaya saw a horse move away from the herd and come nearer to the camp. The horse was Steps High! The herders didn't seem to notice the lone horse, or maybe the sun blinded them when they looked her way. Kaya ran behind the tepees and into the sagebrush beyond the camp. She stopped there and whistled softly. Her horse raised her head and came closer.

Before Kaya could reach her horse, a man strode up beside her, a rawhide rope in his hand. Angrily, he struck Kaya's legs with the rope and gestured for her to get back to the camp. As she turned to go, she saw him put the rope bridle on Steps High's lower jaw. Confidently, he leaped onto Steps High's back and rode away from the camp.

Kaya watched her beautiful horse galloping swiftly across the plain. *If only I could jump on your back and race away from here!* she thought.

The man kicked Steps High until she was running flat out. Her shadow flew at her heels. Then she began to buck! The man whipped her with his quirt and sawed at the rope bridle in her mouth. He dragged the horse's head around and rode her in a circle.

When he managed to subdue her, he rode her back toward camp and whipped her harder. Blood stained the lather on her neck and shoulders.

Kaya wanted to cry out, *Stop!* But she could do nothing to protect her horse—she was a slave.

When Kaya was sent into the thickets to gather

firewood, she sometimes took Speaking Rain along to help carry back the heavy bundles. The slave boy was sent for wood, too. Kaya thought he was about her age, and she wanted to know more about him. But when she came close, he frowned and turned away. Kaya knew he must be ashamed to be doing the work of women. Kaya didn't follow him—these times were her only chance to talk freely with Speaking Rain.

"The hunt will soon be over," Kaya said one morning. "They have almost as much dried meat as the pack horses can carry."

"Aa-heh," Speaking Rain sighed. "It's getting colder, too. Soon they'll start back to their country."

"If only we could escape before they take us farther away," Kaya said.

"Aa-heh!" Speaking Rain agreed.

"But how can we?" Kaya asked. "We'd have to go when it's dark, and at night I'm tied to Otter Woman."

"Could you cut the thong?" Speaking Rain asked.

"I can't reach the knife in her pack," Kaya said.

"But I'm not tied up," Speaking Rain said. "I'll find the knife and give it to you."

"Aa-heh!" Kaya thought a moment as she wound a

thong around the armful of dry branches that Speaking Rain held.

Speaking Rain was quiet, too. "Even if you cut yourself free, I'd never keep up with you on the run," she said slowly. "You'll have to go without me."

Kaya winced at the thought. "I'd never do that!" she said. She'd gotten her sister into this, and she couldn't leave her here as a slave.

"You *have* to leave me." Speaking Rain's voice was firm "You must escape so you can bring others back to get me."

Kaya pressed her fingertips to Speaking Rain's lips. "Don't say that! How could I go without you?"

"Because it's our only hope," Speaking Rain said.

Kaya lifted a bundle of wood onto Speaking Rain's back and took the second bundle onto her own. "But even if I escaped, could I get to Salmon River Country before snow falls?" she asked.

Speaking Rain was quiet for a moment, thinking. "Could you take your horse?" she asked. "You would travel much faster on Steps High."

"They're sure to see me if I try that," Kaya said. "I'd have to slip away on foot. But if I go on foot—"

Her head was spinning. "I don't know what to do. Help me."

"Think," Speaking Rain said. "If Kautsa were captured, what would she do?"

Kaya blinked. She knew the answer to that. "Kautsa would try to escape."

"Aa-heh," Speaking Rain said. "We must start hiding some of our food for your journey."

As they trudged back to the camp, Kaya's mind raced with questions. *How can I leave my sister behind? What will happen to Steps High?*

Then a more terrifying thought came to Kaya: *What if I escape, but I'm captured again? What would the enemies from Buffalo Country do to me then?*

❋◆❋

When Kaya came back to the camp from scraping hides that day, she saw the skinny slave boy tending a fire. There were burrs in his hair, and his only clothing was a ragged breechcloth and worn moccasins.

As she came near him, he motioned for her to stop. He glanced around, then with his hands he threw her the words, *Do you speak sign language?*

Kaya had learned how people talked with gestures when they couldn't speak each other's language. She answered with her hands, *I speak sign language.*

What tribe are you? he signed.

She pointed to herself, then swept her hand from her ear down across her chin. *I am Nimíipuu,* her hands said. *What tribe are you?*

I am Salish, he signed. Then he ducked his head because others came near.

Kaya went on to the Otter tepee, but her thoughts were on the boy. Her people had many friends among the Salish. Nimíipuu often fished and traded with the Salish. Some had even married Salish men and women. Perhaps she and this boy could find a way to help each other.

The next time she had a chance, she picked up some sticks and took them to where the boy was building a fire. Placing the sticks by his feet, she crouched beside him. Would he frown and turn away again?

Instead, he met her gaze—maybe he, too, had been thinking they might help each other. She threw him the words, *What are you called?*

I am called Two Hawks, he signed.

She signed to him, *I am called Kaya.* "Kaya," she said out loud.

He narrowed his eyes and said slowly, "Kaya."

She nodded. Then she had an idea. Perhaps she and Two Hawks could escape together. Two would have a better chance to make it back to the Buffalo Trail and over the mountains than one traveling alone. Would he come with her?

And could she trust this boy? She wished she could know him better before she risked telling him her plan—he might betray her to the enemies in the hope of being rewarded with more food.

Kaya watched for a chance. It came when she and Two Hawks were sent to bring cooking water from the river.

When Kaya was sure no one could see them in the reeds by the river, she signed, *How long have you been a slave?*

I've been a slave for a long time, he answered. *I was captured in a raid on our village. I don't know where my family is, or even if anyone is alive.*

Kaya glanced over her shoulder. They were still alone, but it wouldn't be long before others came here for water. This could be the only chance she'd have to tell him her plan. She'd have to take the risk. *Pay attention to me!* she signed. *I'm going to go to Nimíipuu country. Soon. Come with me to my family!*

His dark eyes bored into her. Then he threw her the words, *I want to go to Nimíipuu country with you.*

Though his solemn expression gave away nothing, she realized he understood! *We will need hides. We will need food*, she signed.

He shook his head. *No! Let's go now!*

Kaya frowned. *This foolish boy!* she thought. If he acted recklessly, he'd put them both in danger. Didn't he know they'd have to wait for a dark night when they couldn't be seen? Didn't he realize they must plan ahead if they were to make it back safely? *Be patient!* she signed. *I'll give you a signal.*

Now! he repeated. Then he pointed to the horse herd not far downstream.

Kaya looked. Men were separating a few horses from the herd. Other men were tying bundles of buffalo hides onto the backs of the horses. She saw that Steps High was one of the horses carrying a load of hides. *What are they doing with those horses?* she signed.

I understand their words a little, he signed. *They are going to trade those horses and hides to another hunting party. Then they'll leave for Buffalo Country. Soon! We must run away now!*

Kaya's mind was whirling—Steps High was going to be traded away! Even now the men were riding off with the loaded horses. Steps High tossed her head and whinnied. She trailed behind the others as if she knew she was being taken far away from Kaya.

Grief was a knife in Kaya's chest as she watched her beloved horse disappear over the rise. Two Hawks was right—they must escape soon or be taken much, much farther from home country.

Kaya bit her lip. How could she bear to leave her sister, and lose her horse as well?

Escape!

CHAPTER 7

Toward last light, the clouds turned red and the west wind blew more and more strongly. Kaya smelled the scent of rain in the wind. She heard small birds sing the high, whistling notes that meant a storm was on the way. By dark it would be raining hard, and everyone would stay inside the tepees with the door flaps closed. The storm would give her and Two Hawks a chance to escape.

When she saw lightning spike down from the clouds, she went to find him. He was banking the fires with ashes. She caught his eye and signaled to him, *Go! Tonight! Meet at the big tree!*

Soon rain lashed the tepees and thunder shook the earth. The dogs huddled down with their heads buried in their tails. Everyone, except for a lone guard, gathered inside. Otter Woman tied Kaya's leg to hers and settled down under several hides to sleep out the storm.

Kaya waited until she was certain everyone slept soundly. Then she whispered in Speaking Rain's ear, "The knife—in the pack beside the door."

Kaya felt Speaking Rain slowly inching herself away from their sleeping place. If she made any sounds, the wail of the storm covered them. After what seemed a long time, Kaya felt Speaking Rain's hand on hers, then the knife in her palm. Gently, Kaya began to work the knife against the rawhide thong—there, she'd cut it! She forced herself to lie still a while longer to be sure Otter Woman hadn't felt anything.

At last, Kaya eased herself away. To deceive Otter Woman if she woke, Speaking Rain took Kaya's place beside her.

Quickly, quietly, Kaya dressed, slid the knife into her bag, and folded up a sleeping hide. She put the little bag of food they'd saved into her bundle, too. Then her courage almost failed her—how could she leave her sister? She clasped Speaking Rain's hand. Speaking Rain squeezed back. Their touch was a vow that they'd be together again. Kaya dragged herself on her stomach under the edge of the tepee until she was outside in the howling storm.

The camp was shrouded in darkness and the rain blew sideways. Kaya didn't see the guard—maybe he was checking on the horses. She crept, keeping low to the ground, until she left the tepees behind. Then she began to run as she had never run before. She sped, wet sagebrush stinging her legs, until she made out the big cottonwood towering over the woods. Was Two Hawks there? Had he been able to escape, too?

As Kaya skidded down the slope toward the big tree, she slipped. She was on her hands and knees when she heard Two Hawks call softly from the bushes, "Kaya?" Never had her name been more welcome to her!

She didn't see the boy until he was right in front of her. In a flash of lightning, she saw that he carried a bundle and wore leggings he must have stolen from a raider. He beckoned for Kaya to follow, then started running across the open plain.

They ran westward into the wind. They had to cover as much ground as they could. As soon as it was light, the raiders would discover that their captives had run off. They'd follow swiftly on horseback. Kaya and Two Hawks must be well away and hidden by then.

All night they ran through lashing rain, but before first light the storm had passed over. Behind them the gray sky shimmered like an abalone shell. They ran along a rocky outcropping until they found a shallow opening beneath an overhang. Two Hawks dragged tumbleweeds over their tracks to cover their trail. Then they spread a hide under the rocky shelf, lay down on it, and covered themselves with the other hide. Two Hawks pulled a tumbleweed into the opening to shield them. Kaya thought she was too frightened to sleep, but in only a moment she fell into a black slumber.

A hand pressed over her mouth woke her. Who held her down? A raider? Then she realized it was Two Hawks signaling her not to speak or move. She heard distant hoofbeats, then the sound of horses running not far from where they lay. Scouts had followed them! Scarcely breathing, she pressed herself against the earth. The hoofbeats became fainter and disappeared. Kaya and Two Hawks had hidden themselves well. But would the scouts find them on their return? The boy must have been thinking the same thing. *Stay still!* he signaled to her.

All day they lay under the ledge. Slowly the light faded and night returned. The enemy scouts hadn't come back. Perhaps they'd given up their search, but there was no way to know. Kaya and the boy would have to be on the lookout every moment so they could see without being seen.

At last Two Hawks signaled to her, *Let's have a look around.* They crept out of their hiding place like prairie dogs out of a burrow. They ate some of their dried meat and sipped rainwater from a hollow in a stone. Then they made their way to the top of a low ridge and paused there to get their bearings. The moon seemed to float up out of the dark lake of waving prairie grasses. The stars were low and bright.

Kaya had been told many stories about the stars to help her find her way. She gazed up at the vast star-map shining above them. She saw the group of stars called the Seven Duck Sisters. But she concentrated on the star that never moves, the North Star, called Elder Brother. With Elder Brother as a guide, she calculated the way west.

Follow me! she signaled to Two Hawks. He shook

his head. Again she motioned for him to follow her, but he stayed put.

Does he think I can't read the stars? Kaya thought. She stamped impatiently and started walking. Before she'd gone more than a few steps, he came after her. Oh, she hoped she wouldn't lead them astray. If she made a mistake in her directions, they wouldn't be able to find the Buffalo Trail.

All night they walked into the wind, which was rising and getting colder. They were near the foothills now, but they would never be able to discover the Buffalo Trail in the dark. They would have to chance moving by day if they were to find it. But first they must rest for a while. When the morning star appeared, Kaya signed to Two Hawks, *We need a lean-to for shelter.*

Enemy scouts might still be looking for them, so Kaya chose a spot hidden deep in a thicket. With the knife, she cut several branches from a pine and leaned them together to make a frame. Then she cut an armful of thick, short branches.

Help me, she signed to Two Hawks.

His lips turned down and his eyes were slits.

Building a shelter is the work of women, he signed. *I won't do the work of women anymore!*

Don't you want to get warm? Kaya signed. *Come on, help me.*

You work, Two Hawks signed. *I'll keep a lookout.* He turned his back on her.

Kaya wove branches into the frame until the shelter was completed. She crawled inside, with Two Hawks right behind her. There was room enough for them to sit upright and eat the last few bites of their food. Kaya chewed slowly. Her belly ached with hunger and her legs shook with fatigue. As they wrapped up in their hides, her mind was filled with worries. Would they manage to find the trail? Could they cross the mountains before snow blocked the pass? Despite her exhaustion, sleep was a long time coming.

Kaya woke to full sun and the sound of geese. When she crawled out of the lean-to, the last grasshoppers of the season sprang up around her. Two Hawks stood grimly gazing up at the flock of geese flying south. Did he know their flight meant snow could be on the way?

Hunger made Kaya dizzy—surely Two Hawks

was hungry, too. She pointed to the dark mass of the foothills ahead. She knew there would be fish in the streams running through the hills. *Let's get some fish,* she signed. *Follow me!*

Two Hawks glowered at her. *Men lead and women follow. You follow me!*

Kaya huffed in exasperation. But she decided not to fight with him—maybe he wouldn't be so disagreeable after they got something to eat.

Soon they were deep in the foothills. Kaya kept looking back, but she saw no signs of enemy scouts. Perhaps they were already on their way to their own country in the east. Before her, the Bitterroot Mountains seemed to reach up to the sky. Snow already lay on the highest ridges. Kaya clutched her hide around her shoulders and shivered. She and Two Hawks didn't have much time. But she was so tired and hungry that her legs wobbled. She needed food and water, and she needed rest. *We must stop here,* she signed.

Two Hawks frowned. *We must go on!*

I can't go on, she signed.

He looked at her hard, his jaw set. *We have to go*

on! he signed. Then he walked off as if he didn't care whether she followed or not.

If this skinny boy can keep going, then so can I! Kaya thought. She caught up with him, but they made slow progress. The woods were full of windfall trees they had to climb over. Twigs tore at Kaya's face and arms, and often she stumbled and fell. Then she heard the sound of a stream. Was this the stream that led to the Buffalo Trail? *We'll rest here and fish tomorrow,* she signed.

Two Hawks turned to her with a sullen expression. *Don't tell me what to do. My father is a warrior. Someday I will be a warrior, too.*

Right now you're only a boy! she signed. *And I know better than you.*

You're not the leader, he signed. *I am! I say we go on!*

Anger flared in Kaya's chest. It had been her idea to escape. If it hadn't been for her, he'd still be a captive. She was the one who had gotten them this far. She knew they'd never make it home if they didn't guard their strength carefully. *I say we build a shelter and rest!* she signed.

Two Hawks screwed up his face in a scowl. *I am*

not your slave! I am no one's slave anymore! I do as I choose!
He turned on his heel and started running alongside
the stream. In a moment he'd broken through some
bushes and disappeared.

Kaya was so upset that her heart was beating like a
drum. How could this boy be so foolish! Should she let
him go on alone, or try to catch up with him again? She
knew they'd be safer if they stayed together, whether
he thought so or not—and she didn't want to face the
night alone. So, against her will, she started plodding
wearily upstream.

Kaya ducked under branches and climbed over
rocks. When she smashed her head against a cedar
limb, she went to her knees in pain. *Let him go on if he
wants,* she thought. *I need to rest.* Crawling on her hands
and knees, she started to move under the cedar tree to
sleep.

Her hand touched something warm and furry.
What was it? She pushed back the branches and looked.
It was the body of a fawn that an animal had killed. She
knew that cougars hunted elk and deer in these woods.
This was a fresh kill—the cougar that had made the kill
must be nearby. Surely it would come back for its meal.

But if the cougar came upon a running boy, it might think that he was more prey and go after him.

Kaya's first thought was to get away from the kill and hide—let Two Hawks look after himself! Then she thought of the magpie feather in her bag. She'd kept that feather to remind herself that she must think of others before herself. She got to her feet and hurried upstream.

Around the bend she saw Two Hawks ahead of her on the pale, sandy shore. He was crouching at the edge of the stream, drinking from his cupped hands. When he heard her coming, he glanced her way. And as he did, she saw the flash of a cougar leaping down from an overhanging limb!

On the Buffalo Trail

 ook out!" Kaya cried. Two Hawks spun onto his side, and the cougar landed on the sand beside him. Kaya ran splashing up the stream, shouting and flapping her deer hide at the cougar. It clawed and bit at Two Hawks's arms and shoulders. Kaya lunged forward and pounded her fist into the cougar's nose. With both hands, she grabbed handfuls of sand and threw them into the cat's eyes.

Blinking and snarling, the cougar released Two Hawks and began to back away. It was a thin, young cat with a lot of scars. Showing its teeth, it turned tail and retreated into the woods.

Two Hawks yanked off his deer hide. Kaya motioned for him to let her see the wounds on his arms. She washed away the blood and exposed the scratches, which were not deep. The deer hide he

wore—and Kaya's quick action—had saved him from
deeper slashes.

Kaya knew how to stop the bleeding. Although
it was almost last light now, she found the plant
called *wapalwaapal*, good medicine for his wounds.
She silently offered a prayer of thanks as she made
a poultice of the leaves and packed it onto the cuts.

Then she sat back on her heels and drew a deep
breath. *We must look out for each other,* she signed. *You
and I are not enemies.*

No, we are not enemies, Two Hawks signed.

We have to stay together, she added. *We have to help
each other.*

He nodded, his eyes downcast. *You did a good thing
for me. How do you say "good" in your language?*

"Tawts!" she said at once.

After a moment, Two Hawks repeated, "Tawts.
Tawts, Kaya."

When light came again, Kaya and Two Hawks
made their way up the stream, looking for a good
place to fish. Kaya's breath clouded at her lips.
During the night, a skin of ice had formed along
the shore. How much longer would snow hold off?

Here the stream widened into a basin before tumbling farther down. This was a good place to catch trout or mountain whitefish.

Kaya untied a piece of fringe from her skirt to use as a sniggle. She lay on her belly by the pool and dangled the fringe in the water. Fish would think the sniggle was food and bite into it. If she was quick, she could flip the fish onto the bank.

Two Hawks tugged a piece of fringe from the side of his leggings and lay down near her. He dangled the fringe in the water and waited. Almost at once, a fish bit the fringe. Expertly, he flipped a large trout onto the stones.

Soon Kaya felt a tug on her sniggle. With a flick of her wrist, she flipped another trout out of the stream and onto the bank. Good—they had enough for a meal.

I'll build a fire, Two Hawks signed.

Kaya watched him choose a sharp stick for a fire drill. He put the point of the drill into a hole in a dry branch. Then he rubbed the stick between his palms until tiny sparks fell onto dried moss. Soon a little flame burned, which he carefully fanned into a fire.

Kaya silently thanked the trout for giving themselves to her and the boy for food. Then she cleaned
the fish and placed them on sticks by the fire to cook.
When the fish were done, she and Two Hawks sat by
the fire and ate them. She licked every bit of oil from
her fingers. Never had anything tasted more delicious
than this meal they'd made together.

As Two Hawks made a fire bundle to save the
coals of their fire, a fine, cold rain began to fall. *Hurry!*
Kaya signed. They had to find the Buffalo Trail before
it was hidden by ice and snow.

As Kaya and Two Hawks made their way uphill,
the cold rain turned into sleet. Kaya pulled her deer
hide over her head, but the sleet made it hard to see.
She thought they'd been following the stream that
would lead to the Buffalo Trail, but nothing here
looked familiar.

After a time, the stream they followed was
nothing more than a small creek racing down the
mountainside. Bighorn sheep leaped across ledges
above them. Slipping on icy stones, Kaya and Two
Hawks struggled upward. At last they reached the
top. Two Hawks gave her a hand, and she climbed

up onto a trail that ran along the ridge.

The trail split around fallen trees—a path made by people on foot. Hoofprints were everywhere along it, too. *It's the Buffalo Trail!* she signed to Two Hawks. Her heart lifted—then she felt a stab of loss again. *If only Speaking Rain were with us!* she thought.

Up here the wind was bitterly cold. Kaya and Two Hawks put their heads down and started along the trail. Kaya saw horse droppings and the remains of fires, but the marks weren't fresh ones. With winter coming, travelers had already left the mountains for shelter in the warmer valleys. But Kaya knew enemies used this trail, too. *Keep a lookout!* she signed. How terrible if enemies should catch them now, with home country only a few sleeps away!

Wet and shivering, the two of them worked together to build a small lean-to against a rocky outcropping far off the trail. Because there was no water up here on the ridge, they scooped handfuls of sleet to suck.

If I had a bow and arrow, I could get us food, Two Hawks signed.

But there's hardly any game up this high, Kaya

answered. *We'd still have nothing to eat.*

Then she saw that some pines were marked where people had stripped back the bark to get at the soft underlayer. The underlayer was food for both men and horses when they had nothing else to eat.

Here is food, Kaya signed. She began stripping back the bark with her knife.

As Kaya and the boy ate, wolves began to howl to each other across the ridges. Kaya and Two Hawks huddled together for warmth like puppies.

At first light, ice crystals glittered on frozen branches that rattled in the wind. Kaya and Two Hawks lined their moccasins with moss to keep their toes from freezing. Their fingers were blue and their teeth chattered when they took to the trail again, but during the night the sleet had stopped.

Even though she was cold, this old, worn trail comforted Kaya. She felt the presence of the people who had passed this way before her.

After walking a long time, they came to a large cairn, a pile of stones that marked a special place. People had built many cairns along the Buffalo Trail. The cairns marked sacred places where spirits were very strong. Two Hawks went on down the trail to scout their way, but Kaya stopped by the old cairn.

As she stood there, she thought she heard the voices of spirits. Were they reminding her that her name meant "she who arranges rocks"? Were they telling her to build another cairn at this sacred place?

She couldn't lift big stones, so she collected small ones and piled them up until she'd made a mound. She wanted to offer something of her own, too. She opened her bag and looked inside. There was the magpie feather she'd kept. Since Magpie was her nickname, she tucked the feather under the top stone of the mound.

❖

All day, and all the next day, they climbed higher and higher. Kaya and Two Hawks looked around as they walked, often glancing up at the birds and clouds for signs of the weather. Suddenly, Two Hawks pointed to a large tree far off the trail. There, high in the tree, was a platform of branches. A bundle was tied onto the platform. Had hunters left food here for their return journey?

Two Hawks climbed up the tree to see. He came

down with a rawhide bag slung over his shoulder. The rawhide was from the top part of a tepee, darkened from smoke that made it waterproof. *This is a Salish bundle,* he signed. *My people hunt on this side of the mountain. My people hid this food here!*

Eagerly, they opened the bag. Inside were dried camas cakes and pemmican, a mixture of dried meat, grease, and dried berries. They sat under the tree to eat the tasty, nourishing pemmican. This unexpected find would give them the strength to push on.

They were hurrying up along the trail when Two Hawks signaled for Kaya to halt. *Look,* he signed. *Do you know that country?*

Kaya looked where he pointed. In the far, far distance she could see what seemed to be a stretch of prairie. Was that the prairie where her people sometimes dug camas bulbs? If it was, they were closer to home country than she'd thought. *Soon we will be with my people!* she signed.

Come on! Two Hawks answered. *Let's get a better look!*

Kaya's heart was light as they scrambled up off the trail to a place where they could see more clearly. From up here, the prairie looked like a brown blanket laid over the land. Two Hawks was even more eager than she to see it. He climbed a tall pine until he was almost to the top, leaned out, and shaded his eyes.

With a sharp crack, the branch he stood on snapped under his weight! Crying out with surprise, he pitched backward and fell. He crashed down through the branches. With a thud he hit the rocky ground and tumbled down the hill on the far side. He cried out again, this time in pain.

Kaya rushed down to him. Clutching his ankle, he lay on his side. She crouched and saw a lump on his ankle. When she touched it, he gasped.

She handed him a stick to use as a cane. He seized the stick and tried to rise, but when he put weight on his injured leg, he collapsed in pain. He tried again, only to fall a second time. His face was wet with sweat from his struggle. *My ankle is broken,* he signed.

Kaya bit her lip. She knew she wasn't strong enough to carry Two Hawks more than a little way. Maybe he could crawl a little way, too. But if he couldn't, how would they get out of the mountains?

She hugged herself. What should they do now?

The cold wind whipped about them, and last light was coming soon. They needed a shelter and a fire.

Kaya collected dry twigs and sticks and handed Two Hawks the fire bundle he'd made. Grimacing in pain, he unwrapped the coals in the fire bundle and set about building a fire. As he worked, she gathered branches and built a lean-to shelter. How she wished for many, many hides to make the shelter windtight! They had the Salish food, but Two Hawks was in too much pain to eat. His teeth chattered and his whole body shook. His eyes were wide with fright.

How could Kaya help him? She lay down against his back and put her arms around him to keep him as warm as possible. Still, he trembled violently, though he would not cry.

Then Kaya thought of the lullaby that Speaking Rain had sung. Kaya put her lips close to the boy's ear. "*Ha no nee,*" she sang very softly. "*Ha no nee.*" When at last he did sleep, he groaned over and over.

Somehow, Kaya slept, too. When she woke, she opened her eyes to a white world. Snow was falling thickly. Glittering flakes filled the air and drove into the opening of the lean-to. Snow covered the ground and weighed down the branches of the trees.

Two Hawks tried again to rise, only to collapse onto his side. Kaya knew she couldn't carry him on the steep and icy trail. She'd have to leave him here, hurry on, and try to reach her people. If he stayed in the lean-to with some food, perhaps he wouldn't freeze before she returned with help.

She crawled out of the lean-to and looked up toward the ridge. Drifts and blowing snow were all she could see. By now, snow would have covered the Buffalo Trail as well.

As she stood in the whirling white, she saw a woman standing under a pine tree on the slope. The woman was tall and strong, like the woman named Swan Circling. She wore an elk hide over her shoulders, and snow glistened in her braids. Light surrounded her, like the sun shining on ice. While Kaya watched, the woman turned and strode up toward the ridge, looking back over her shoulder from time to time.

Kaya clutched her hide around herself and followed. Upward she climbed, wet snow falling onto her shoulders from pine branches when she brushed against them. Snow fell onto her head and into her eyes. She wiped her eyes, and when she looked again, the woman was gone. In her place, a wolf stood gazing at Kaya with yellow eyes. She saw the black tips of its raised ears and its thick, yellow-gray coat. It watched her intently as she climbed up to the ridge.

When Kaya reached the top, the wolf trotted slowly down the slope on the other side. It paused now and then and looked back at her, as if waiting for her to come along. Was the wolf a wyakin? Kaya hurried after it, and then, with a bound, the wolf leaped down into the trees and disappeared.

"Wait for me!" Kaya whispered. With the wolf gone, the woods seemed much lonelier.

As she searched the hillside for the wolf, she saw something moving. She ducked out of sight behind a tree and peeked around through the veil of snow. Farther down the hillside, she made out a horse and a rider wrapped in a buffalo hide. Enemy? Friend? The rider led a pack horse and rode a large bay stallion. Could it be Runner, her father's horse? Could Toe-ta be here in the mountains?

Kaya went skidding down the hill, snow flying up around her feet. "Toe-ta!" she cried as she went.

"Kaya!" he called back, and turned the horses uphill to meet her.

Then he was leaning over, lifting her up, putting her onto his horse in front of him. He wrapped her in the warm buffalo robe he wore and held her close. "Daughter, you're alive!" he said. "And Speaking Rain? Is she alive, too?"

Kaya put her face against Toe-ta's chest. It was like a dream to be in his strong arms again.

"Speaking Rain's alive, but she's a slave of our enemies," she said. "I escaped with a Salish boy, but he broke his ankle. He's over that hill!" She pointed.

Toe-ta took fur-lined moccasins from his pack and put them on Kaya's cold feet. He pulled out another buffalo robe, wrapped it around Kaya's shoulders, and set her behind him on Runner. Leading the pack horse, they started back over the ridge to get Two Hawks.

Kaya clung tightly to Toe-ta's back. "How did you find me?" she asked.

"We searched and searched but found nothing," Toe-ta said in his deep voice. "Then two sleeps ago, a scout came to our hunting camp on the Lochsa. He'd come down from the Buffalo Trail to the river because snow was coming. He told us he'd seen a new cairn at a sacred place along the trail. The cairn was made of small stones—ones someone with small hands might choose. Hands like yours, Daughter.

"The scout said a magpie feather was stuck into the little cairn. I thought of your nickname—Magpie. I left our hunting camp and came up here to search for you. But if you hadn't come running, I wouldn't have found you in this snow. Were you watching the trail?"

"I didn't know where the trail was—" Kaya began, but then she stopped herself. She wouldn't speak of the spirit woman who led her away from the lean-to. She wouldn't speak of the wolf who had brought her in sight of the Buffalo Trail and Toe-ta, either. If the wolf was a wyakin, she would not tell anyone until the proper time came.

So much had happened to Kaya—how could she tell all of it? Where would she start? "Toe-ta, the raiders traded away my horse," she said.

"She's a good horse," he said slowly. "Perhaps you'll see her someday."

"And Two Hawks—can we help him get back to his people?" she asked.

"We'll help the boy join his people when the snow melts and it's time to dig roots again," Toe-ta assured her.

Kaya pressed her face to Toe-ta's back. She closed her eyes tightly and forced herself to say what she had to admit. "It's my fault Speaking Rain's a slave," she whispered. "I thought of my horse before I thought of Speaking Rain's safety. But I made a vow I'd bring her back to us—somehow."

Toe-ta reached back and pulled the buffalo robe closer about Kaya. "We'll do all we can to find Speaking Rain, but you must not blame yourself that you were taken captive," he said. "You were taken far from home, and you've endured much. But, Daughter, you are alive and well! Let us give thanks to Hun-ya-wat that you're with us again!"

Runaway Horse!

CHAPTER 9

Kaya was happy to be back in Nimíipuu country, but she felt as if she had two aches in her chest. Once ache was a sharp-edged gratitude that she was with her people again. But the other was a stab of grief that Speaking Rain was still a captive. Kaya had promised that they would be together again, but where was her sister now? If Kaya could find her, how could she save her? And would she ever see her beautiful, beloved horse again?

It had been many sleeps since Kaya had returned to the winter village. Now she knelt on a mat in the lodge and leaned over the baby named Light On The Water, who lay in her *tee-kas*. "Tawts may-we!" Kaya crooned to her. "Are you unhappy this morning?"

Light On The Water gazed steadily into Kaya's eyes,

but her mouth trembled and turned down as if she was about to cry.

Kaya stroked the plump, warm cheek. "Are you wet? Is that what you're telling me?" she asked. She loosened the lacing of the buckskin that wrapped the baby and pulled it away from her feet and legs. The soft cattail fluff that cushioned the baby's bottom was soaked. Kaya pulled it out, dried the baby, and placed fresh fluff underneath her. She squeezed one of the baby's little toes and kissed her forehead. Light On The Water smiled now. "Tawts!" Kaya said as she laced up the covering again.

Running Alone, Kaya's young aunt, put her hand on Kaya's shoulder. "Won't you make the lacing just a little tighter?" she asked. "We're going to ride out to gather wood for the fires, and I want my baby very safe."

Kaya tightened the lacing, then carried the baby out of the lodge. The day was chilly, and Light On The Water's breath was a small cloud at her lips. When Running Alone had mounted her horse, Kaya handed her the baby. Running Alone slipped the carrying strap of the tee-kas over her saddle horn and gazed down at her smiling daughter. "She likes your gentle touch," she told Kaya.

"She's so easy to care for," Kaya said. "Not like my little brothers. Look, they think I can't see them hiding behind that tree." She pointed at the two sets of dark eyes gleaming through the branches of a pine. "Boys, let's go riding!" she called to the twins, and they came running, clutching robes of spotted fawn skin around their shoulders. Like all Nimíipuu children, they loved to be on horseback.

Kaya helped one twin climb up behind her older sister, Brown Deer. Then Kaya mounted a chestnut mare and lifted up the other twin. As she waited for the other women and children to mount, she glanced up toward the north. The foothills of the distant mountains were already white-robed with snow, but here in Salmon River Country the earth was still brown and bare. Each winter, Kaya's band came to these sheltering hills to make their winter village. They put up their lodges near the banks of the stream and stayed until spring, when it was time to move up to the prairie to dig nourishing roots and bulbs for food.

Kaya pulled her elk robe more tightly around her

shoulders. Even dressed warmly in fur-lined
moccasins, leggings, and her robe, Kaya shivered in
the chill of winter. She remembered how cold—and
hungry!—she and Two Hawks had been as they made
their way over the Buffalo Trail. Now she and the boy
were safe again, fed by the meat and warmed by the
hides of animals that had given themselves to her
people. But Two Hawks had broken his ankle on the
trail, and it was slow to heal. He sat alone and home-
sick all day.

Kaya thought of the sadness Two Hawks carried
as the group of riders set off single file. After a time,
they came to a bowl-shaped canyon where trees grew
thickly. The children ran to play, and the women
fanned out along the creek to gather wood. A girl
named Little Fawn and some boys were climbing
aspen saplings and swinging to and fro on them.

"Magpie, fly into the trees with us!" Little Fawn
called to Kaya.

Magpie! Kaya winced. She tried to ignore that awful
nickname.

"Not now!" she called back. "I'm going to look for
more fluff for the baby."

She glanced toward Light On The Water and
Running Alone, who was tethering her horse to a tree.
The baby, lulled by the rocking ride, napped in her
tee-kas on the saddle horn. Taking a twined bag, Kaya
started for the stream after the other women.

Suddenly, a sharp crack echoed across the canyon.
Kaya whirled around—the branch Little Fawn was
pulling on had broken off. Little Fawn jumped to the
ground. The branch slashed down like a spear and
struck the rump of Running Alone's horse. The startled
horse reared up in alarm and broke her tether. Wild-
eyed, the panicked horse began to bolt down the
canyon, the baby in the tee-kas still hanging on the
saddle!

"Stop! Stop!" Running Alone cried out. She ran
after the galloping horse.

Kaya ran, too. The fleeing horse was already
halfway down the canyon and heading for the
narrow opening and open country beyond. The tee-kas
bumped against the horse's shoulder with each
plunging step. Would the baby be tossed off? Light On
The Water could be hurt badly—or killed!

Near the canyon opening, the young woman named

Swan Circling came rushing from the woods.
Dropping her robe behind her, she ran swiftly to cut
off the horse's escape. She reached the opening of the
canyon first and spun around to face the galloping
horse, which was thundering straight at her. Taking a
stand, she spread her arms wide, like an eagle in flight.

Would the horse run her down? Swan Circling
stood her ground. Right in front of her, the runaway
skidded to a halt. The horse snorted and tossed its
head, flinging lather onto both Swan Circling and the
baby.

Swan Circling seized the horse's reins. She held the
horse firmly in place as Running Alone came rushing
to get her baby.

Running Alone lifted the tee-kas from the saddle
horn and clutched it to her chest. "My little one!" she
cried, kissing her baby's face over and over. "You saved
my baby, Swan Circling! Katsee-yow-yow! I can never
thank you enough!"

Kaya came running right behind her aunt. She
reached to take hold of the reins, too, and stroked the
horse's neck and shoulder to calm her.

"I saw you step in front of my horse, but how did

you get her to halt?" Running Alone asked. "She could have run right past you—or right over you!"

"I didn't think of that," Swan Circling said. "I wanted her to stop, and she did. Is your baby all right?"

Light On The Water was grinning. She thought the bouncing, runaway ride was a game.

Swan Circling glanced at Kaya, who was still stroking the horse's lathered neck. "You seem to have a way with horses," she said approvingly. "She's quieting down. Will you lead her back now?"

Kaya held the reins of the uneasy horse securely as she and Swan Circling returned to the others. As they walked, she studied Swan Circling's calm face. Kaya had been curious about Swan Circling ever since she'd married Claw Necklace and joined the band. And now Kaya remembered that the woman who appeared to her when she was lost on the Buffalo Trail had looked like Swan Circling. Had that vision been a sign that they would be friends? Kaya hoped so. She wished she could become as strong as this brave young woman who hadn't even flinched when a horse charged straight at her!

❋◆❋

Later that day, Kaya sat with other girls and
women at one end of a lodge that several families
shared. Many layers of tule mats and hides covered
the lodge. Parfleches and piles of hide blankets were
stacked along the bottom to keep out drafts. The
women unfolded the hides they'd tanned in the
summer and set about making moccasins and clothes
and carrying cases. They took out the hemp cord
they'd twisted and wove baskets and bags. They made
their clothes beautiful with fringe and beads and quill
decorations. Kaya loved working with the others in the
warm winter lodge.

Kaya watched Brown Deer stringing a necklace
of beads made from shells. From time to time, Brown
Deer ran her fingers lovingly across the beads. The
necklace was for a man—and Kaya guessed her sister
was making it for Cut Cheek. The two had danced
together last summer, and soon they'd see each other
again when he came with other neighboring villagers
for the winter gatherings. Each day now, Brown Deer
combed her hair and dressed it with fragrant oil so

it would grow long and silky.

Eetsa was finishing a large twined storage bag, one of the many, many gifts they would give to family and friends when they came to visit.

Kautsa was weaving a small hat. Kaya watched her grandmother's expert work closely—because the hat was for her. Kaya would wear it in the spring when she went to dig roots with the other girls and women. She loved the red zigzags that Kautsa worked into the design.

Kaya put aside the basket she was weaving and picked up her sister's worn buckskin doll. Speaking Rain had carried her doll everywhere she went. With her sister gone, Kaya kept the doll close to her. As she adjusted the doll's dress, she discovered a tear in her back, a bit of deer-hair stuffing poking out. She decided to mend it and have it ready for Speaking Rain when she was with them again.

Kaya wanted to care for the doll because she feared she hadn't taken good care of Speaking Rain. *If I were as strong as Swan Circling,* Kaya thought, *I'd find a way to get my sister back.*

"Kautsa, may I ask you a question?" Kaya asked.

"Aa-heh, you may ask me anything," Kautsa said. A slight smile crinkled the corners of her eyes. "Ask— then I'll decide if I want to answer you."

"You're teasing," Brown Deer said, laughing. "You always answer us!"

"It's true," Kautsa said. "I've always answered your questions—so far! What do you want to know?"

Kaya threaded her bone needle with a bit of sinew and began stitching the tear in the buckskin doll. "I want to ask about Swan Circling. What makes her so— different?"

"Different?" Kautsa said. "You must be asking me how Swan Circling came to be a warrior woman. Now, there's a story!"

"Can you tell us?" Brown Deer asked eagerly.

Kautsa nodded. Her fingers were busy as she twined the brown hemp with the yellow beargrass. "Swan Circling came to live with us when she and Claw Necklace married, three winters ago. We all saw that she was a strong girl, eager to help. Then . . ." Kautsa paused and held the hat she was weaving above Kaya's head to check the size. The many strands of cord trailing from the hat tickled Kaya's nose.

"Then?" Kaya prompted her grandmother.

"Then?" Brown Deer echoed. "What happened then, Kautsa?"

Kautsa put the hat back into her lap and began to work on it again. "Then Swan Circling went with her husband on a hunting trip to Buffalo Country. While they slept one night, enemies attacked them!"

"To steal horses, as they did with us?" Kaya asked.

"Not to steal horses," Kautsa said. "They came to fight—or to show their courage just by touching our warriors! Our men rushed from the tepees to defend themselves. Claw Necklace hurried into the skirmish. But in his eagerness to fight, he left behind his bow and arrows."

"He didn't have any weapons?" Kaya asked.

"Aa-heh, he was in great danger!" Kautsa said. "Instead of running for cover with the other women, Swan Circling picked up his weapons and ran after him into the fight. Arrows flew around her. One even singed her arm, but it didn't pierce her flesh. She gave her husband the bow and arrows so he could fight well, and then she tended our wounded men. She was never wounded by arrows, though a few tore her dress."

"Did Swan Circling tell you this?" Kaya asked.

"She would never speak of her bravery," Kautsa said. "It was Claw Necklace who told us what had happened. After our men won the fight, they gave Swan Circling an eagle feather for her bravery—a very high honor, as you know."

"I know she goes to battles," Brown Deer said. "She brings fresh horses to the riders whose horses have been hurt."

"So she does," Kautsa said. "Swan Circling has brought many things to us. You were with her when she saved Running Alone's baby, weren't you, Kaya?"

"Aa-heh, Kautsa," Kaya said. "I saw it all."

"Then you know she's fearless," Kautsa said. "I believe she wouldn't hesitate to fight a grizzly bear! There's only one sad thing . . . "

Brown Deer stopped stringing beads and looked up. "What sad thing?" Brown Deer asked.

"As you know, Swan Circling doesn't have any children. That's sad, don't you think?" Kautsa asked.

"It would be very sad not to have any children," Brown Deer said slowly, as if she were imagining how she'd feel if she were Swan Circling.

"But she and her husband are young," Eetsa broke in. "There's still plenty of time for them to have children."

"Aa-heh," Kautsa agreed. "There's time for children. And they'll be strong, like her, I'm sure of that." Then she tapped Kaya's hand. "I'm glad you mended your sister's doll, Granddaughter."

Eetsa rose to her knees and peered into the cooking basket. "We need some water so we can cook our meal," she announced.

Right away Kaya got to her feet to go fetch the water. She caught up with Little Fawn on the trail to the stream. Like Kaya, Little Fawn carried a large water basket, but she was limping. "Did you hurt your-self when the branch broke?" Kaya asked. "Maybe you climbed too high."

Little Fawn winced at each step, but she shook her head. "It's nothing. I've jumped out of trees much higher than that."

Other women and girls were drawing water at the stream. Kaya saw Swan Circling a little way down-stream, leading a spotted mare. As the mare drank, Swan Circling dampened a bundle of leaves and tied it onto the mare's back. Kaya went downstream to her side. She'd been eager to see Swan Circling again, but now that she stood beside her, she didn't know what to say. She stroked the mare's flank. "This is a pretty one," she said. "Has she got sores on her back?"

"Aa-heh," Swan Circling said. "The men saw her rolling in a patch of sage to heal herself. They asked me to make a poultice of the sage for her."

"The spots on her rump remind me of my horse, Steps—" Kaya stopped, afraid to go on for fear her voice would break.

Swan Circling glanced at her with concern in her eyes. "You miss your horse, don't you?" she said. "I just saw the boy who escaped with you."

Kaya leaned out and dipped her water basket into the stream. "Two Hawks can't put weight on his broken ankle yet," she said. "He has to be patient."

"You're right," Swan Circling said. "It takes time for bone to heal. But he looks lonesome and grumpy."

"That's because he doesn't like to be patient!" Kaya said.

Swan Circling laughed. "That's the kind of boy he is! It's good you were with him when you escaped.

You're a dependable girl, I can see that. You two were very strong to run away and find your way back. It's too bad he's unhappy here with us."

Kaya's cheeks burned with pleasure at this praise from the woman she admired so much. To keep Swan Circling from seeing that she was blushing, Kaya turned her head.

Little Fawn was standing on the shore a little way upstream, a basket of water in her arms. When Kaya looked her way, Little Fawn lifted her chin and narrowed her eyes. "Magpie flew back to her nest!" she said, and limped away. Was she jealous of the praise Kaya had been given?

"Magpie?" Swan Circling said. "Is that your nickname, Kaya?" She patted the mare's rump and took her lead rope.

"They call me that sometimes," Kaya said.

Swan Circling gave Kaya a searching look. "Some nicknames dig into us like bear claws," she said. "As you grow older, they don't hurt so much. Will you remember that, Kaya?"

"Aa-heh," Kaya said. "I'll remember."

"Tawts!" Swan Circling said with approval. She

started to lead the mare back to the men who tended the horses.

Kaya bit her lip as she watched Swan Circling walking back to the herd. Swan Circling had offered her good advice about her nickname. But, of course, she didn't know that Kaya had gotten it last summer because she'd gone off to race her horse instead of taking care of her brothers. Whipwoman had scolded Kaya, saying she must learn to think of others before she thought of herself. If Swan Circling knew that, she'd certainly regret calling Kaya strong—or dependable. And if she knew it was Kaya's fault that she and Speaking Rain had been taken captive, would Swan Circling have any respect for her at all?

Lessons from a Basket

he next day Kaya went to find Two Hawks, who was sitting outside one of the lodges.

Sometimes he sat there all day without moving, an antelope hide wrapped tightly around him. "I know you can't walk yet, but I bet you can ride," Kaya said to him.

Two Hawks frowned—he understood only a few words of her language.

Kaya used her hands to speak to him. *Do you want to ride with me?*

"*Wah-tu!*" he said. He'd learned the word for "no" right away. He shrugged, his lips turned down. With his hands he signed, *Leave me alone!*

But Kaya wasn't going to leave him alone. She'd been thinking about what Swan Circling had said— Two Hawks was unhappy. Kaya's father had promised they would help Two Hawks get back to his people in the spring, but that time was a long way off. Since Two Hawks had been here, he hadn't smiled once. Kaya couldn't help him get home any faster, but she could be a better friend to him.

She signed to him, *You can't just sit there. I'm going to get a horse for you.*

"Wah-tu!" he said again and shook his head.

But the word "no" was a challenge to Kaya. She went to get the chestnut horse she rode and another gentle mare. She put light rope bits on them and led them back to where Two Hawks sat, his chin on his knees. "Two Hawks!" she called to him. She threw him the words, *Let's go! Let's ride!*

He shook his head angrily. *I can't ride,* he signed. *My ankle is broken.* He pointed to the splint that was bound to his ankle.

You can do it! she signed. *I'll help you,* she added, though she wasn't sure how she could get him onto the horse.

Two Hawks grimaced as if he was determined to prove her wrong. He pushed to one foot, supporting himself with a crutch made from a cottonwood branch.

Kaya led the gentle mare close to him. Two Hawks looked at Kaya darkly, as if to say, "What now?"

She thought a moment. Then she signed to him, *Put your knee in my hands. I can lift you onto the horse.*

Two Hawks looked at the horse, then back at her. He shook his head. Did this stubborn boy think she wasn't strong enough to lift him? She clasped her hands and held them by his injured leg. After a moment, he gingerly placed his knee in her grip and grabbed the horse's mane with both hands. "Now!" Kaya said. She lifted, he threw his good leg over the horse's back, and he was mounted.

Kaya studied him. He wasn't grimacing with pain. In fact, he looked pleased. She climbed onto her horse and beckoned for him to come with her. She'd thought of something Two Hawks could do while his leg healed. She threw him the words, *We have to find an elderberry stick so you can make a flute.*

❀◈❀

Overnight it had grown colder. A sharp wind whined around the lodge where Kaya and other children were dressing themselves after their morning swim. But the lodge was warmed by five fires in a line down the center, smoke rising through the long opening at the top. Eetsa and the other women were already cooking a morning meal because there was much work to do that day.

Kaya knew that soon friends and family would come from other villages nearby for the new year celebration, when the short winter days begin to grow longer again. People would share their news and give each other gifts. They'd feast and tell stories and honor Hun-ya-wat, who made the seasons and held them in balance.

Today the women were putting up another lodge, one large enough to hold everyone for the feasts. When Kaya joined them, she saw Swan Circling helping to raise one of the long lodge poles and set it onto the frame of tepee poles. Kaya thought the framework looked like the backbone and ribs of a skeleton of a huge horse. After the women completed the frame, they would cover it with tule mats and hides. Kaya helped other girls carry the rolled-up mats and place them near the builders. She kept Swan Circling in sight, hoping to have a chance to talk with her again.

With the lodge finished, Kaya followed Swan
Circling to another lodge where women were
preparing more food so that there would be enough
for the visitors. Eetsa and Running Alone were making
pemmican. With a stone pestle, they were pounding
dried deer meat in one of the large mortars. When
one of the women got tired using the heavy stone
pestle, they traded places. Kaya thought the steady
thump, thump, thump sounded like a heartbeat.

Swan Circling joined the women, and Kaya went
to peek at Light On The Water, who was snug in her
tee-kas.

"Would you give my baby a piece of this dried
meat?" Running Alone asked Kaya. "She's getting a
new tooth, and she needs something to chew on."
She turned back to breaking strips of the meat and
putting the pieces into the mortar to be ground fine.

Kaya broke off a bit of the meat and held it to
Light On The Water's lips. But the baby pressed her
lips shut tightly, her eyes merry as if she and Kaya
were playing a game. "Isn't she precious!" Kaya
exclaimed. Then she glanced at Swan Circling.
Kautsa had said it was sad that she had no children yet.

Did she mind that Kaya was making a fuss over the baby?

Swan Circling was using the large pestle. Her strong arms gleamed with sweat from the hard work. "When I saw you girls in the stream this morning, I thought of the time when I was your age," she said when Kaya caught her eye. "Do you like to swim?"

"Aa-heh!" Kaya said.

"So do I," Swan Circling said. "I come from a place where the Snake River joins the Big River. My friends and I swam every chance we got. My mother called us the Fish Girls. Someday I'll show you my favorite places to dive from the cliffs, Kaya."

"You're always thinking of the future, aren't you?" Eetsa said to Swan Circling. "Many times I've heard you say 'someday this' or 'someday that.'"

"It's true," Swan Circling said. She smiled at Eetsa, who was her good friend, and passed her the pestle. Then she wiped her face with the back of her hand. "Do you often think of what's to come, Kaya?"

Kaya was thinking that no one had ever asked her as many questions about herself as Swan Circling did. Kaya liked that. "I think of seeing my horse again,"

Kaya said. "Mostly I think of getting my little sister back. But I don't know how I can do that."

"When a way opens, you'll be ready," Swan Circling said with confidence. "I saw you riding with Two Hawks yesterday. I don't know how you persuaded him to get on a horse, but you did! He looked as if he was in a much better mood. You have a strong will, Kaya, and I'm glad you think of the needs of others."

Kaya gently rocked the baby in the tee-kas. Lulled by the motion and the voices of the women, Light On The Water was falling asleep. Oh, how Kaya wanted to be the girl Swan Circling believed her to be. And how she feared she wasn't!

❈◆❈

"Pay attention, I have something to tell you," Kautsa said to Kaya and the other girls and women who were gathered around making baskets. On these long winter evenings, when the wind howled like a pack of wolves, they stayed close to the glowing fires in the warm lodge. Kautsa never missed a chance to teach the children with stories or legends. She was a

wonderful storyteller and acted out the different parts
with her hands and her low, musical voice.

Kautsa held up a basket made of cedar bark.
"Here's a basket traded to me by one of our friends
to the west," she said. "She told a story to go with the
basket, a story about how Cedar Tree taught them
basket making," she continued. "Listen, and I'll tell it
to you."

Kaya sighed with pleasure. She glanced over her
shoulder at Swan Circling, who was twining a basket
as she listened with the others. Swan Circling caught
Kaya's glance and nodded, as if to say, *Yes, I love to listen
to stories, too.*

"It was so, my children, that a long time ago all the
animals, plants, trees, and creatures could walk and
talk the way that people do," Kautsa began. "In those
long-ago days, Gray Squirrel was a girl, like all of you.
But she was a little slow in her thoughts, and she was
clumsy, too. Day after day she sat all alone under a
cedar tree. Cedar Tree began to feel sorry for Gray
Squirrel and decided to help her. He couldn't allow
her to grow up without learning what a girl needs to
know.

"Wise old Cedar Tree sent Gray Squirrel to pick beargrass, dry it, and put it into bundles. Then he told her where to find dyes and how to cut and dry his own roots to make cedar strips. When she had all the materials she needed to make a basket, he taught her how to weave it. She was so proud of her work! But Cedar Tree told her to dip her basket into the stream. Was it woven tightly enough to hold water? When water ran out of her basket, Gray Squirrel hung her head and cried.

"'Don't cry, little girl!' Cedar Tree said." Kautsa made her voice strong and low, the voice of a wise old tree. "He told her she'd have to practice and practice in order to make a basket successfully. Then he sent her out to look for designs to weave into her basket.

"Gray Squirrel went looking. Rattlesnake gave Gray Squirrel the zigzag design on his back. Mountain gave her the design of his peaks and valleys. Grouse gave her the design of his track marks. Stream gave her the design of his waves. To find all these designs, Gray Squirrel had studied the world so closely that now she was much, much wiser.

"Gray Squirrel wove a beautiful basket with all of

the designs she'd been given. And when she dipped it into the Big River, her basket didn't leak! Now she was very proud of herself—and Cedar Tree was proud, too. But he told her that she should set down her basket in the woods and leave it there. She must give her basket back to the earth to show that she was thankful for what was given to her.

"Gray Squirrel didn't like that one bit! But Cedar Tree insisted that if she didn't give away the basket, she would never be a good weaver. And she had to make five little baskets and give away those, too! She must learn to work for others, not just for herself.

"Coyote was coming up the Big River at that time," Kautsa continued, finishing the story. "He saw Gray Squirrel's fine basket, and he was impressed with it. He told her that soon people would come into that part of the world. Already people were so close that Coyote could hear their footsteps. He said that from that day forward, the women of that land would be well known for their cedar baskets. And it's so, isn't it?" Kautsa spread her strong, gnarled hands on her knees.

One little girl gazed up at Kautsa longingly. "Tell us another story?" she asked.

Kautsa smiled. "Instead, why don't you make a little twined basket like the one Kaya is working on? I'll start it for you, and she'll help you if you get into trouble. Won't you, Granddaughter?"

"Aa-heh, Kautsa," Kaya said. She would do anything that her grandmother asked of her. But she hoped Swan Circling had heard how quickly she agreed to Kautsa's request—she wanted her friend to think well of her. It seemed that no matter what Kaya was doing, she had Swan Circling on her mind.

⊗◆⊗

The next morning as Kaya stepped out of the stream where the girls had taken their morning swim, she saw Swan Circling beckoning to her. The frigid air made Kaya feel like running and jumping with energy. She pulled her elk robe around her and hurried to meet Swan Circling.

"Tawts may-we!" Kaya said.

"Aa-heh, tawts may-we, Kaya," Swan Circling said. "That story your grandmother told last night set me thinking. I have something I want to show you. Would you like to work with me today?"

"Aa-heh!" Kaya said. "If Kautsa says I may, I'll work with you."

"Run and ask her then," Swan Circling said. "I'll be in the lodge."

After Kautsa said that Kaya could work with Swan Circling, Kaya joined her again. Swan Circling was kneeling on a mat in the crowded lodge. Kaya knelt at her side and watched her untie the flaps of a large parfleche painted with triangle designs in red, blue, green, and yellow. "Your grandmother's story reminded me of a basket I made when I was a little girl—my very first one," Swan Circling said.

"My first was awfully lopsided," Kaya said, "but I gave it to Kautsa anyway."

Swan Circling lifted out her special ceremonial dress and moccasins from the parfleche and set them aside. Then she took out a little brown twined basket and handed it to Kaya. "You can see that my first basket's lopsided, too."

Kaya smiled at the lumpy little basket. She liked to imagine Swan Circling as a girl with small hands and big ideas—a girl just like Kaya. She was happy to be sitting at her friend's side. "Didn't you give your first basket to your grandmother?" she asked.

Swan Circling nodded. "Aa-heh, I did. After she died, it was given back to me. I'm glad. This basket taught me many lessons."

Kaya turned it over. With her fingertip she traced the weaving. "Was one of the lessons to make your twining tighter?"

Swan Circling smiled. "Aa-heh, to pull the cord tighter was one thing I learned. But that wasn't all— I learned about patience, too. I was a very bold, headstrong little girl. I thought that there was nothing I couldn't do!"

"But you can do everything, can't you?" Kaya asked.

Now Swan Circling laughed. "Of course I can't!" She put her warm hand on Kaya's knee. "You see, I'd been watching my grandmother weave her baskets, and I was sure I knew how. I decided I was going to make a beautiful one just like hers. I got my basket started, but I made mistake after mistake. Finally, I had this pitiful little thing to show her."

"What did she say about it?" Kaya asked.

"She thanked me and said I'd made a start. But I

expected more praise than that," Swan Circling
admitted. "I remember I was pouting. I asked her why
she hadn't corrected my mistakes, as if the lumps in
my basket were her fault! Then she told me, 'Everyone
has to have her own experience. Everyone has to learn
her own lessons.' Little by little I understood that to
make a mistake is not a bad thing. But I should be
wise enough not to make the same mistake again—
and again."

Kaya understood that Swan Circling wasn't
speaking now of basket making—she was speaking
of life.

This was a chance for Kaya to tell Swan Circling
about how she'd gotten her nickname and why the
enemies were able to capture her and Speaking Rain—
and about her guilt for escaping without her sister.
She could tell Swan Circling the truth. "I've made
mistakes, too," Kaya began. "I . . . "

Swan Circling waited for her to go on.

But then Kaya lost her nerve. What if she told Swan
Circling the truth, but her friend lost respect for her?
If she did, she wouldn't seek out Kaya anymore. No,
Kaya couldn't risk losing Swan Circling's friendship.

"I left holes in a basket I was making," Kaya said in a determined voice. "But my grandmother showed me right away so I could do a better job." She handed back the clumsy little basket.

Swan Circling repacked it with the other things and tied the parfleche. "Is something troubling you?" she asked Kaya. "There's a crease right here." She put her fingertip between Kaya's eyebrows.

Kaya didn't meet Swan Circling's gaze. "No, nothing's troubling me," she said.

Still Swan Circling waited. After a moment, she put the parfleche back on the stack against the lodge wall. "Maybe we've done enough talking," she said. "Come, let's pack up the pemmican and put it into storage."

A Sick Baby

uring the night a light snow fell. Kaya was sweeping it away from the outside of the lodge when she heard a soft sound that gently rose and fell—the sound of a flute. She cocked her head. Someone was playing sweet, winding notes that sounded both happy and sad at the same time.

The melody made Kaya think of a warm spring breeze blowing in the depth of winter. Had Two Hawks finished the little flute she'd helped him begin? Was he playing it? When she'd swept the ground bare with the piece of sagebrush, she hurried to find him.

She found Two Hawks in the lodge near the door. He was sitting with an older boy named Runs Home, who held a flute to his lips. The sweet music Kaya had heard was the older boy's skilled playing. Kaya knew

Runs Home liked to serenade girls on long summer evenings.

When Two Hawks saw Kaya, he raised his flute to his lips and blew. A squeak! He blew again. Another shrill squeak and then a squawk!

Runs Home frowned. He took the flute from Two Hawks and compared it to his. He showed Two Hawks that the slit he'd made in the top was too small and the holes in the side were too large.

Two Hawks seized his flute and shoved it out of sight under a parfleche. He folded his arms over his chest and gave Kaya a fierce look of anger and disappointment.

Since Two Hawks had been with her people, he'd put on some weight and he looked much healthier, but at that moment he reminded her of the skinny, bitter boy she'd first seen in the enemy camp.

"Can you help him find another elderberry stick?" Runs Home asked her. "He can learn to make a good flute if he'll let me work with him."

Kaya threw Two Hawks the words, *Come with me. We'll find another stick.*

Two Hawks turned his head. Kaya thought that

if his ankle was healed and he could run away from them, he would.

You can't make something perfect the first time you try, she signed to Two Hawks. *You have to practice! I'm going to get horses for us so we can find another stick for you.*

"Will he go with you?" Runs Home asked her.

"He did before," she said firmly. "He will again. I'm sure of it."

Listen to me, Runs Home signed to Two Hawks. *I'll teach you some things.*

Two Hawks looked closely at Runs Home, then at Kaya. He set his jaw and shrugged. Then he got to his feet and hobbled outside right at Kaya's heels, as if he was relieved that she and Runs Home hadn't let him quit on his first try.

❈◆❈

Kaya and Brown Deer were helping Kautsa take wrapped camas cakes from a storage pit when a crier came riding through the village. "Friends are arriving! Get ready for them!" he called out. They all stopped what they were doing and gathered to welcome their visitors.

A northeast wind, the coldest one, blew fine flakes of snow. Kaya shaded her eyes as she watched the horizon. Soon she saw a dark line of horses and riders come over the snow-covered rise and descend to the village.

What could be better in this cold season than the warmth of greeting friends and family! Everyone hugged and smiled and talked and handed around gifts. Men, women, and children crowded inside with their belongings until all the lodges were pleasantly full.

Kaya caught sight of Cut Cheek standing with Toe ta and *Pi-lah-ka*. He'd come with the others from a winter village nearby. She'd forgotten how handsome Cut Cheek was, with his broad forehead, flashing eyes, and high cheekbones, a scar on one of them.

Would Brown Deer hurry to greet him, as others were doing? He was looking around the gathering. Kaya searched the crowd, too—where was her older sister?

Then Kaya saw her. Brown Deer was standing modestly by the doorway of their lodge. Her cheeks were burning, as if she knew Cut Cheek was looking her way. Then she raised her eyes to his. Something passed between them like a shiver of heat lightning. Kaya smiled to herself and thought, *Someday soon Cut Cheek will wear the necklace Brown Deer is making!*

Kaya's aunt from a nearby village greeted her with a strong hug and a kiss. "Scouts told us about your capture and escape," she said. "We're so glad you're well!"

"Did your scouts have any news of my sister?" Kaya asked.

The smile left her aunt's face. "No one has any news of her," she said. "Of course, no one can cross the Buffalo Trail now. Our enemies must have taken her back to their country with them."

Biting her lip, Kaya turned away.

Swan Circling touched Kaya's arm. "Will you help me carry these baskets of food?" she asked Kaya gently. "We have so much to do for the gathering tonight."

When night came on, Kaya and the others dressed in their best clothes and entered the ceremonial lodge for the new year gathering. This was the shortest day of the year—and the darkest. The clouds had cleared, and stars shone in the sky, where the new moon, thin as a fish bone, had risen. Four big tepees had been put together to make this lodge, but soon the large space was crowded with people of all ages.

Several men held a drum made of hide. The fires in the center of the lodge cast their light on the walls, and the air smelled sweetly of cedar boughs and tule mats.

When everyone was in the lodge, To Soar Like An Eagle raised his hand to get attention. He wore a feathered headdress and a painted hide shirt decorated with porcupine quills. He was a very respected old chief with white eyebrows and a low, powerful voice that came from deep in his chest. Kaya watched his lined face as he spoke.

"Hun-ya-wat has made this night longer than all the others," To Soar Like An Eagle said. "In this darkest time, let us reflect on the days that have gone before and on the days that lie ahead. It is time to renew life."

The drummers began, filling the night with drumbeats that echoed back from the surrounding hills. After the drumming, men and women began to speak of births and deaths and of the gifts Hun-ya-wat had given them in the past year. They told of good deeds and acts of bravery. They gave thanks for successful hunts and for ample fish and roots and berries. Together they prayed that all might keep their minds and hearts pure so there would be enough food in the year to come.

Kaya listened closely to the prayer songs. She looked at her parents and grandparents standing near her. Firelight played over their solemn faces. Brown Deer, too, was sober and thoughtful. Even the twins, such lively little boys, seemed to be listening closely to the singing.

Two Hawks, who couldn't understand the words, gazed steadily at the others as though he understood everything from their serious expressions.

Kaya could see Swan Circling standing with her young husband, Claw Necklace. Her dark eyes reflected the firelight, but her thoughts seemed far away, as if she was thinking of the future again.

Kaya considered her own life over the past year. She had much to be thankful for, but she had many regrets, too. Her good and bad feelings mingled like the streams of smoke rising from the fires.

When Kaya glanced again at Swan Circling, she realized what was troubling her most tonight—she hadn't yet told her friend how she got her nickname or how her disobedience had gotten her and Speaking Rain captured. She hadn't been brave enough. But until she did, Swan Circling wouldn't really know her.

Kaya closed her eyes. *Hun-ya-wat, make me honest and strong in character,* she prayed silently. *Help me face life with an honorable, truthful, and strong will.*

When the prayers came to an end, it was time for the midnight feast. Women brought out steaming salmon broth followed by bowls of mashed roots and berries. As Kaya watched the preparations, she felt a quiet, calm resolve in her heart. Her prayer had given her courage. She would tell Swan Circling everything— and as soon as possible.

❀◆❀

Kaya watched for a chance to speak with Swan Circling, but with all the visitors crowded into the lodges, they were never together. After several days, the visitors left for their own villages. Now, surely, Kaya could take Swan Circling aside and talk with her.

One morning Kaya was piling wood beside the cooking fires when Running Alone hurried over. "Would you look after my baby for a little while?" Running Alone asked Kaya. "I'm troubled about her. I want to find Bear Blanket and ask her for help."

Kaya was worried as she followed Running Alone through the lodge to her sleeping place. Bear Blanket was a powerful medicine woman who had cured many, many sick people. Light On The Water must be sick, or Running Alone wouldn't be looking for the medicine woman's help.

Light On The Water lay in a hide swing hung from the lodge poles. Kaya leaned over her. The baby's face was flushed, and each time she drew a breath she coughed. Tiny beads of sweat covered her forehead and cheeks. Her eyes were open, but she didn't gaze up at Kaya. She didn't seem to see anything at all.

When Running Alone hurried off, Kaya placed her finger in the baby's hot little hand. Light On The Water didn't tug at it, as she usually did. "Are you sick, little one?" Kaya whispered. "There's help for you. You won't be sick for long."

Soon Bear Blanket came through the door of the

lodge. She was an old, gray-haired woman, but her back was as straight as an arrow. Kaya knew that Bear Blanket always kept her mind and body clean so she would be ready to help those who needed her. Her animal spirit helper was a grizzly bear. Long ago she had received medicine power—the power to heal— from this wyakin.

Bear Blanket carried a medicine bundle in one hand. Swan Circling followed right behind her.

Running Alone motioned for Kaya to stand aside so that Bear Blanket could see the baby. The old woman studied the baby's face and bent over to listen to her coughing. Then she spread her hands over the baby's head and began to sing one of her medicine songs.

As she sang, she passed her hands up and down over Light On The Water's body. Kaya saw the baby's eyelids tremble and shut, then open again when she coughed harder.

Bear Blanket drew Swan Circling aside and spoke to her, then went back to her singing.

Swan Circling frowned. "She wants me to bring her the inner bark of a special tree to boil for a healing drink," she said to Running Alone. "I'm going to get my horse and go after it now."

"But it's very cold," Running Alone said. "The northeast wind is blowing again. Will you be all right?"

"I can't wait," Swan Circling said. "Your baby needs the medicine now."

Running Alone put her hand on Swan Circling's arm. "Then hurry!" she urged her. "Kaya will round up your horse for you while you get your blankets and your knife."

Kaya threw a deerskin over her shoulders and grabbed a rope bridle. Her breath was a white plume at her lips as she ran out to the herd grazing near the village. She found Swan Circling's white-faced horse, placed the bridle on her lower jaw, and rode her back to the lodges.

Swan Circling was wearing otter-skin leggings and mittens and had her elk robe around her. She held her beautiful saddle of wood and painted rawhide. Kaya reined in the horse and slipped off. She put on the saddle and reached under the horse's belly for the cinch. Already Swan Circling was hanging her bags from the saddle horn.

"Cinch it snugly," Swan Circling told her. "I'm going

to ride as fast as possible. Bear Blanket said the baby is very sick." She tested the saddle cinch with her weight, then swung up. "Good work, Kaya. I'll be back before last light. Watch for me." She urged her horse forward and, in a few strides, was running full out across the frozen ground.

"I'll watch for you!" Kaya called after her. But the wind snatched away her words.

All day Kaya stayed with Running Alone and her baby. Bear Blanket sang her medicine songs, but the baby only coughed harder and harder. Her little face was red, and her eyes screwed shut with her effort to breathe. Kaya watched her anxiously—did the baby have the terrible sickness of blisters that the men with pale faces had brought to the land? Kaya was afraid to ask.

As the light began to fade, Kaya went to watch for Swan Circling's return. At dusk there were no colors in the valley. The river was a shining black curve, like a snake, and the trees were black slashes against the white snow. Under dark clouds, a hawk rode the wind in slow, wide turns. *Where is Swan Circling?* Kaya thought. *Why doesn't she come back?*

Then she saw a horse appear in the trees at the far end of the valley. Kaya ran up the hillside a little way to get a better look. The horse had a white face—Swan Circling's horse. Kaya caught her breath in relief. But as the horse came closer, out of the trees, Kaya saw that it was limping as though it was hurt—and that it had no rider.

Gifts from Swan Circling

Kaya watched as Claw Necklace, Toe-ta, and two other men saddled their horses and rode off to search for Swan Circling. Kaya couldn't believe that anything bad could have happened to her friend—she was so young, so strong. Maybe she'd fallen off her horse, and it had run away from her. Surely she was coming home on foot and the men would soon meet up with her. In the meantime, here was her bag—still hanging on the saddle horn.

Kaya ran with the bag to find Bear Blanket. The medicine woman was with Running Alone and her baby, who lay gasping in the baby swing. Bear Blanket opened the bag and took out a handful of bark. "This is the good medicine I asked for," she said.

"Tawts!" Running Alone exclaimed. "I knew Swan Circling wouldn't fail us."

Kaya dug her fingernails into her palms as she gazed down at the baby's red face and dry lips. Would blisters soon break out on her cheeks? Her people had never seen the men with pale faces, but their sicknesses had killed many Nimíipuu. "Tell me," she asked fearfully, "does the baby have the bad sickness that kills?"

"Not that," Bear Blanket said quickly. "She has a weakness in her chest."

Kaya unclenched her fists. "Will the medicine help her, then?"

"I'll make a healing drink with it," Bear Blanket said. "Soon she'll breathe more easily. Go rest, Kaya. There's nothing you can do now."

Kaya was warm under a blanket of woven strips of rabbit fur, but she couldn't sleep. Her thoughts were with Swan Circling, who was somewhere in the darkness and the cold wind. Perhaps she'd built herself a lean-to for shelter, as Kaya had done when she escaped from the enemies. Or maybe, any moment now, Swan Circling would come walking into the lodge with Claw Necklace. She had to be all right!

Kaya slept fitfully. Before first light she awoke to a cold draft on her cheek. She pushed up onto her elbow.

A few people were stirring in the lodge, and someone
had pulled back the covering of the doorway. Had
Swan Circling returned? Kaya crawled from underneath her blanket. She saw Eetsa leaving the lodge,
a torch in her hand. Kaya pulled her elk hide robe
around her shoulders, followed Eetsa to the door, and
peeked out.

The moon had already set, and the sky was turning
gray. In the space between the lodges, Eetsa joined a
group of men and women. Kaya saw Kautsa, Pi-lah-ka,
and other elders wrapped in their robes. Toe-ta was
speaking to them. And now she made out Claw
Necklace walking toward the lodges. He carried
something. Kaya blinked. Then she realized it was
Swan Circling that Claw Necklace held in his arms.

Kaya couldn't get her breath. No!—Swan Circling
would be all right! She would be! Kaya pulled her robe
over her head and hid her face in it.

In a moment she felt firm hands on her shoulders.
She lifted her chin and looked up into Kautsa's face. In
the gray early light, her grandmother looked very old
and very tired. "Our men found her body beside the
stream," Kautsa said quietly. "It seems her horse broke

through thin ice and stumbled, and she was thrown off. Her head struck a boulder, and the blow killed her." She opened her arms and took Kaya into her warm embrace.

Through her tears, Kaya heard Kautsa's gentle voice at her ear. "She was full of light and love," Kautsa said. "It's hard to let her go, but we must help her spirit journey on."

❈◆❈

Kaya walked in a daze after Swan Circling's death. She felt as if a jagged hole had been torn in her heart. Mixed in with the pain of her friend's death was another pain—one of regret. Oh, why hadn't she quickly called up the courage to tell Swan Circling everything? Now it was too late.

Everyone in the village grieved and mourned for Swan Circling. They comforted each other with gentle words and tried to console Claw Necklace, too. Runners took the bad news to neighboring villages. Though it was the heart of winter, one runner volunteered to travel all the way to the Big River to tell Swan Circling's family.

None of Swan Circling's family lived close enough to help with the burial, so the women in her husband's family took charge of all the preparations. They got to work right away. The best hide workers took out fresh white deer hides, clean and unused, to make a new dress and moccasins to clothe the body. Other women prepared food to serve the whole community after the burial ceremony. Some stayed with the body, never leaving it alone, even for a moment.

Kaya stayed close to Running Alone and her baby. The medicine had helped Light On The Water. She wasn't coughing so hard now, and she gazed up at Kaya's face when Kaya rocked the sling and sang to her. Light On The Water didn't need encouragement to sleep, though—she was still weak and listless.

Even when the baby slept, Kaya kept singing the lullaby, "She's the precious one, my own dear little precious one." She was sure Swan Circling was listening. Until her body was buried, her spirit would stay close by.

Kaya was gently rocking the sleeping baby when she thought she heard a canyon wren singing somewhere near the lodge. Kaya cocked her head. Was

Swan Circling sending a message through a bird? Kaya went outside to look for it.

Wrapped in his antelope hide, Two Hawks was standing near the lodge. He still used a stick for a crutch, but he could put more weight on his leg now. He saw Kaya and limped over to meet her. When he was in front of her, he put the little flute he'd been working on to his lips. His cheeks puffed out as he played *tee, tee*—the sweet, descending notes she'd mistaken for birdsong.

"That's a pretty sound," Kaya said. "May I look at your flute?"

He handed it over. His face was solemn, but his dark eyes were lively—she saw that he was proud of what he'd made.

The little flute was well and carefully made, and Two Hawks had smoothed the wood to a gloss. "Tawts!" she said. "Good work, Two Hawks."

"Runs Home helped me," he said. "He's my friend now."

"I see he's helping you with words, too," she said. "You've made a good flute. Now you have to learn to play it."

"I can play!" he insisted. He brought the flute to his lips and blew, his eyes narrowed in concentration. *Tee, tee, tew,* he played. This time he was able to add a third note to the song.

Two Hawks's success lifted Kaya's sad heart a little. His leg was healing, and he was a happier boy now. And it seemed that Light On The Water would get well. These were things to be thankful for in this dark time. Surely Swan Circling's spirit would find comfort in these things, too.

Before first light on the third morning after Swan Circling's death, Toe-ta and other men went to the burial place on a rise above the stream to dig a grave. When they sent word that the grave was ready, everyone gathered in the faint light for the ceremony.

Swan Circling's body and some of her things had been wrapped in clean hides and fresh mats and placed on a horse-drawn travois. Fighting her tears, Kaya followed with the others as the body was taken to the burial place—which faced the east, where the sky would soon brighten.

A medicine man with strong spirit powers led the way. He was a short man with a broad chest and shoulders, and he wore a fur headdress set with mountain sheep horns. At the graveside, he praised Swan Circling's strength, her unwavering courage, and her willingness to help her people. He spoke of everyone's sorrow to lose such a good woman. Then he urged her spirit to travel on.

As the first streak of dawn stained the pale sky, the men placed the body in the shallow grave and covered it with another mat. First the women, then the men stepped one by one to the grave and dropped in a handful of earth. When it was Kaya's turn, she vowed silently, *All my life I'll think of you! I'll strive to be like you, I promise!*

But Swan Circling's spirit wouldn't be able to rest until all of her belongings had been given away or burned. Because Eetsa had been a close friend of Swan Circling, she took charge of the giveaway.

In the lodge, Eetsa placed all of Swan Circling's belongings on a mat. After all the people had eaten the meal the women had prepared, they gathered around the mat. One by one, Toe-ta called them to step forward. With a few words, he gave Running Alone the mortar and pestle. Little Fawn received the

digging stick, and Kautsa a large parfleche. To
Brown Deer he gave a pair of deerskin moccasins. He
gave other women and girls Swan Circling's baskets,
necklaces, shells, and hides until there was nothing left
on the mat by his feet but Swan Circling's saddle.

Then Toe-ta motioned for Kaya to come forward.
She kept her gaze on her moccasins as her father spoke
to her. "Claw Necklace told me his wife admired your
care for horses and your love of them," he said gently.
"He's certain she would want you to have her saddle."

"Katsee yow-yow," Kaya murmured.

Then Toe-ta rubbed his lips with his thumb. He
thought a moment. "She also wanted you to have
something much more important than a saddle,"
he said.

In his deep voice Toe-ta told how Swan Circling
had recently come to him and Eetsa and asked to speak
with them. "She told us she had a dark dream, a dream
of her death," he said. "She wasn't frightened, but she
said that if she should die, she wanted Kaya to have
her name. As you know, her name was hers to give as
she chose. She was fond of you, Kaya, and she spoke of
your special friendship. She believed you would carry

her name well. We accepted her gift to you with gratitude."

Now a very old woman lifted her head to speak. It was her job to remember how everyone was related to each other. "What Kaya's father says is true," she said firmly. "I was there when Kaya's parents accepted the name. I say this is so."

Kaya hugged the beautiful saddle of wood and painted rawhide that Toe-ta had handed her. But as she turned and walked back to her place, her mind couldn't take in the second gift that Swan Circling had given. Her name! That was the greatest gift anyone could give. Kaya's thoughts rushed back and forth between gratitude and doubt. How honored she was to have been given her friend's name! But could she truly be worthy of it? And would Swan Circling have given it if she'd known Kaya's failures? If only Swan Circling were here, for it seemed to Kaya that her friend was the one person who could quiet these racing doubts and fears. But Kaya was alone with her torn feelings.

It wasn't until that night that Kaya could talk with her mother. Eetsa had heated stones in the fire and was putting them into a water basket to boil deer meat.

She stirred the hot stones rapidly to keep them from scorching the basket. Kaya crouched by her side.

"Eetsa, I'm troubled about my namesake," Kaya said, careful not to say the name of the dead out loud.

Eetsa lifted out the cooled stones with a forked stick and put in more hot ones. "What troubles you, Daughter?" she asked.

"I don't think she'd have given me her name if she'd known the mistakes I've made," Kaya admitted. "I never told her about my nickname or how I got myself and Speaking Rain taken captive."

When Eetsa glanced at her, Kaya saw her mother's eyes soften. "But there's nothing to be troubled about," Eetsa said. "She knew about your nickname, but she said it didn't matter to her. And she said it took great strength to leave your sister behind and that you were wise to do so."

"She said that to you?" Kaya asked.

"Aa-heh," Eetsa assured her. "She often spoke about you. She told me she had confidence that you would grow to be trustworthy and strong. And she said you have a generous heart, Daughter—which you do. It's not time for you to use her name yet, but when that time comes, you'll know. Is anything else troubling you?"

Kaya pressed her lips together and shook her head. Her heart was full—she was afraid that if she spoke, she'd burst into tears of both gratitude and relief.

❈◆❈

The next morning, Kaya sat with her little brothers on her rabbit-fur blanket. The twins lay on their stomachs with their chins in their hands. They were watching as she shaped and tied long pine needles to make three little horses.

"Is one of those horses for me?" Wing Feather asked.

"If my brother gets a toy, so do I!" Sparrow demanded. "Don't I, Kaya?"

"Yes, one of these horses is for you," she said, tapping Wing Feather on his nose. "And one's for you," she told Sparrow and tugged his braid.

Kaya put the finishing touches on the little horses and handed one to each boy. "Here they are," she said. "Now you can have races."

"Katsee-yow-yow!" the twins said at the same time.

They seized their toys and scampered with them to the pile of hides where other children were playing.

Kaya cut a small piece of hide and tied it with a bit of fringe onto the third little horse's back—there, now this one had a saddle. Then she wrapped herself in her elk robe and left the lodge without telling anyone where she was going. Since she'd wakened, she'd known what she must do.

The trail to the burial place led around the sides of low hills. Bare trees cast blue shadows on the thin covering of snow. Coyotes hunting rabbits had left tracks in the snow, and she saw the wing print of a hawk that had swooped down for a kill.

On the east-facing side of the hill, she turned off the trail. There were many graves here, marked with rocks. Mourners had left small gifts on some of them. Kaya went to the place Swan Circling was buried and put the little horse made of pine needles on her grave.

"I've been thinking about things," Kaya said softly to her friend. "I want you to know I'm going to live up to your expectations—and that I'm grateful for your trust. And your name. But I hope to get my sister back before I use it, and maybe my horse, too. I want to deserve what you've given me. I want our people to think well of me when they call me by your name."

Kaya looked back at her village. In the cold, only dogs moved between the lodges. Everything was quiet, but soon family and friends would return for the winter Spirit Dances, and the village would be crowded again. She stood a moment more, squinting into the morning light that flooded the long, broad valley, and then she started home.

INSIDE Kaya's World

When Kaya was growing up in the 1760s, her people called themselves *Nimíipuu*. Today they are known as the *Nez Perce*, which is French for "pierced nose." Early white explorers, including French fur trappers, mistakenly believed that all Nez Perce wore shells through their noses and gave them the name.

In Kaya's time, Nez Perce people lived in the forested mountains, grassy prairies, and steep canyons of present-day Idaho, Washington, and Oregon. They traveled with the seasons throughout this vast territory to gather food and to hunt and fish. While traveling, Nez Perces set up temporary camps of small tepees. Then, every fall, the people settled back into their permanent villages in the warmer valleys along rivers and streams.

Wherever they lived, Nez Perce children helped with daily tasks from an early age. They gathered firewood and fetched water. A young girl like Kaya would be learning how to cook food and prepare it for winter. She would learn how to soften animal hides and make clothes from the prepared skins. She would learn how to weave baskets and bags, and she would begin to learn how to build a home for her own family one day.

Nez Perce children spent much of their time with grandparents and elders. They were the main teachers in the community because they had the most patience, wisdom, and experience. Everything in Nez Perce culture was passed on by example and through songs, stories, and legends that Nez Perces learned by heart. Through stories about a character named Coyote as well as other animals, Nez Perce children learned about how—and how *not*—to behave, and the traditions and history of their people. The children had sharp memories!

For children like Kaya, their classroom was the world around them as they learned the skills they needed to survive in the outdoors. They were taught to recognize— and avoid—the markings of dangerous animals such as rattlesnakes and grizzly bears. Girls learned to collect berries and dig roots, and boys were taught to fish and hunt. Children were also trained to be strong. They exercised constantly by running foot races, riding horses, and playing ball games.

Riding and handling horses was a particularly important skill to Nez Perces, who learned to ride when they were as young as three years old. They bred horses for speed, endurance, strength, and sure-footedness. Many of their horses had the striking spotted coats of the horses now known as *Appaloosas*. Horses allowed Nez Perces to travel farther and faster and to carry more goods. Horses were a sign of wealth, but they were also well loved, just as Kaya loved Steps High. The Nez Perce treated their horses with great respect. They honored them with decorated collars and saddlebags and paraded their horses in their finest outfits to show pride in Nez Perce artistry and culture.

GLOSSARY of Nez Perce Words

In the story, Nez Perce words are spelled so that English readers can pronounce them. Here, you can also see how the words are actually spelled and said by the Nez Perce people.

PHONETIC/ NEZ PERCE	PRONUNCIATION	MEANING
aa-heh/ˊéehe	*AA-heh*	yes, that's right
Aalah/Eelé	*AA-lah*	grandmother from father's side
Eetsa/Iice	*EET-sah*	mother
Hun-ya-wat/ Hanyawˊáat	*hun-yah-WAHT*	the Creator
Kalutsa/Qalacá	*kah-luht-SAH*	grandfather from father's side
katsee-yow-yow/ qeˊciˊyewˊyewˊ	*KAHT-see-yow-yow*	thank you
Kautsa/Qáacaˊc	*KOUT-sah*	grandmother from mother's side
Kayaˊatonˊmyˊ	*ky-YAAH-a-ton-my*	she who arranges rocks
Nimíipuu	*nee-MEE-poo*	The People; known today as the Nez Perce
Pi-lah-ka/Piláqá	*pee-LAH-kah*	grandfather from mother's side
Salish/Sélix	*SAY-leesh*	friends of the Nez Perce who live near them

tawts/ta´c	*TAWTS*	good
tawts may-we/ **ta´c méeywi**	*TAWTS MAY-wee*	good morning
tee-kas/tikée´s	*tee-KAHS*	baby board, or cradleboard
Toe-ta/Toot´a	*TOH-tah*	father
wah-tu/weet´u	*wah-TOO*	no
Wallowa/ **Wal´áwa**	*wah-LAU-wa*	Wallowa Valley in present-day Oregon
wapalwaapal	*WAH-pul-WAAH-pul*	western yarrow, a plant that helps stop bleeding
wyakin/ **wéeyekin**	*WHY-ah-kin*	guardian spirit

Read more of KAYA'S stories,
available from booksellers and at *americangirl.com*

❋ *Classics* ❋
Kaya's classic series, now in two volumes:

Volume 1:
The Journey Begins
When Kaya and her blind sister are captured by enemy raiders, it takes all of her courage and skill to survive. If she escapes, will she ever see her sister—and her Appaloosa mare, Steps High—again?

Volume 2:
Smoke on the Wind
Kaya's pup, Tatlo, gives her comfort while she searches for her lost sister and her beloved horse, Steps High. When a forest fire threatens all she holds dear, Kaya must face her greatest fear yet.

❋ *Journey in Time* ❋
Travel back in time—and spend a day with Kaya!

The Roar of the Falls
What's it like to live in Kaya's world? Ride bareback, sleep in a tepee, and help Kaya train a filly—but watch out for bears! Choose your own path through this multiple-ending story.

❋ *Mystery* ❋
Another thrilling adventure with Kaya!

The Silent Stranger
During the winter Spirit Dances, a strange woman appears in Kaya's village. Why is she alone, and why will she not speak? To find out the truth, Kaya must look deep into her own heart.

※ *A Sneak Peek at* ※

Smoke on the Wind

A Kaya Classic

Volume 2

Kaya's adventures continue in the second volume of her classic stories.

ne morning, Kaya heard the crier calling out that a new trader had arrived. He had come from far away, where the Big River flows into the sea. Quickly Kaya's grandfather dressed in his best hide shirt and leggings, wrapped his deer-skin robe over his shoulder, and went to meet the man. Her grandfather was a shrewd trader. He took with him camas cakes, buffalo hides, and bundles of tules, things that people from the coast would be sure to want.

All day Kaya looked forward to Pi-lah-ka's return. Her grandfather would have many stories to tell, and he might have heard something about Speaking Rain. Slaves were sometimes traded to other tribes—could her sister have been traded to people from the west?

Pi-lah-ka didn't ride back for a long time. When he did, there were big packs tied onto his pack horses.

Two Hawks was helping Kaya's father coil up hemp rope for trading. Toe-ta and Two Hawks hurried with Kaya and the others to crowd around Pi-lah-ka. Toe-ta motioned for everyone to be seated. Then Pi-lah-ka opened up a pack and showed them what he'd gotten in trade with the man from the coast.

First, he handed around a few special beads he'd gotten in exchange for a fine buffalo hide.

Kaya held one of the precious beads in her palm. It gleamed a deep blue, as if she held a piece of the evening sky. Oh, it was beautiful!

Out of the corner of her eye, Kaya saw Two Hawks turn to look at the arrival of more new traders riding by with their many pack horses. After a moment, he jumped to his feet.

"Sit, Two Hawks," Toe-ta said sternly to him. "Pay attention to your elders."

Two Hawks sat again. Kaya could see that he was trying to be respectful, but he was almost too excited to hold still.

"Tell us," Pi-lah-ka said. "What's troubling you?"

"I think those traders are Salish," Two Hawks said. "They're hauling hide tepee covers like my people use, and I think I recognize that big black horse. Maybe those men know what's happened to my family. Can't we follow them?"

Toe-ta stood up right away. "Get your horse," he told Two Hawks. "Kaya, come with me on my horse. Let's see if these men are Salish." He put his hand on

Two Hawks's shoulder. "If they are, we'll trade this boy to them for a worn-out moccasin. That would be an even trade, wouldn't it?"

Two Hawks grinned at Toe-ta's joke. Then his glance caught Kaya's, and his smile dimmed. She saw that he was very happy—and also a little sad. Of course, he wanted to get back to his home again. But now he felt at home with her people, too.

The traders were setting up their camp on the eastern edge of the clusters of tepees. Toe-ta signaled a greeting to them as they rode up. But Two Hawks reined in his horse and circled around behind Toe-ta as if he were feeling shy.

A young trader stepped forward, shading his eyes against the setting sun. Toe-ta threw him the words, *This boy is Salish. Do you know him?*

The trader squinted up at Two Hawks and beckoned for him to ride closer. After a moment, the trader shook his head—it had been a long time since Two Hawks was taken captive, and the man didn't recognize the boy.

But Two Hawks recognized him! He slipped off his horse and ran to the young man. Two Hawks threw his arms around the man's waist and pushed his forehead against his broad shoulder. Then they were both laughing and talking at the same time.

When Kaya and her father joined them, Two Hawks turned to them excitedly. "This is my uncle— my mother's brother!" he cried. "He says my parents are alive and well. My sisters are well, too. He'll take me home with him!"

"Tawts!" Toe-ta said. "Two Hawks, ask your uncle to share a meal with us. We have much to talk over with him."

❈◆❈

Eetsa prepared a meal of kouse root mush, berries, and deer meat. Afterward, the men talked. Because Two Hawks spoke both Nimíipuu and the Salish language of his people, he acted as interpreter. Sometimes they used sign language, too.

Kaya closely followed what they said. Two Hawks told of his time as a slave of enemies from Buffalo Country, and of his and Kaya's escape, and how Toe-ta had found them on the Buffalo Trail. Young Uncle told of everything that had happened to Two Hawks's

family while he was gone from them. Toe-ta made
plans to join some Salish men to hunt buffalo in their
country to the east, and they agreed to meet again the
next day to trade with each other.

Then Toe-ta asked about Speaking Rain. Had
Young Uncle seen or heard of his little daughter, a
blind girl? She'd been a captive, too, but she might
have escaped, or been traded. Was there any news
of her?

Young Uncle frowned sadly. *I have not heard of the
girl you describe,* he said with his hands.

Kaya clasped her hands tightly to keep from
crying. But now Two Hawks turned to look her in the
eye. "You helped me and brought me to my family,"
he said to her. "I give my word that I'll try to find your
sister and bring her to you."

Kaya blinked back her unshed tears. Two Hawks
was her friend after all. "Katsee-yow-yow," she said to
him gratefully.

Then Two Hawks and Young Uncle spoke together
for a little while. Two Hawks turned to Toe-ta. "My
uncle gives you his pledge, too," he said. "When it's
time for salmon fishing at Celilo Falls, some of my

people will join your people there. Maybe we'll have
news of your daughter then."

Toe-ta nodded. He threw Young Uncle the words,
Thank you for your help.

Kaya glanced at her mother. Eetsa sat with her head
bowed, her lips pressed tightly together. Kaya saw the
sadness in her father's face, too. She understood that
to lose a child was a terrible thing. And to lose a sister
was terrible as well.

Two Hawks leaned toward Kaya. "I asked my
uncle about your horse with the star on her forehead,"
he said. "He hasn't seen your horse, but we'll be on the
lookout."

"Katsee-yow-yow," Kaya murmured a second time.

About the Author

When JANET SHAW was a girl, she
and her brother liked to act out stories,
especially ones about sword fights and wild
horses. Today, Ms. Shaw lives in North
Carolina with her husband. Their two dogs
sleep at her feet when she's writing.

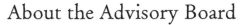

About the Advisory Board

American Girl extends its deepest appreciation
to the advisory board that authenticated Kaya's stories.

Lillian A. Ackerman, Associate Professor, Adjunct,
Department of Anthropology, Washington State University

Vivian Adams, Yakama Tribal Member, former Curator of
Native Heritage, High Desert Museum

Rodney Cawston, Colville Confederated Tribes

Constance G. Evans, Retired IHS Family Nurse
Practitioner and former Nez Perce Language Assistant/
Instructor, Lewis-Clark State College

Diane Mallickan, Park Ranger/Cultural Interpreter,
Nez Perce National Historical Park

Ann McCormack, Cultural Arts Coordinator,
Nez Perce Tribe

Frances Paisano, Nez Perce Tribal Elder,
Retired Educator

Rosa Yearout, Nez Perce Tribal Elder,
M-Y Sweetwater Appaloosa Ranch